Vilho

Vilho

FINNISH FREEDOM FIGHTER

SEQUEL TO JONAS OF KIIVIJARVI

Leslie W. Wisuri

NORTH STAR PRESS OF ST. CLOUD, INC.

Printed in the United States of America by Versa Press, Inc.
East Peoria, Illinois.

Published by
North Star Press of St. Cloud, Inc.
P.O. Box 451
St. Cloud, Minnesota 56302

Introduction

THE FINNISH PEOPLE WITHSTOOD SIX HUNDRED YEARS of oppression from Sweden, and then the Russians took over in 1809. The oppressive yoke became too heavy to bear, and small uprisings started everywhere.

Important among the resistors was a Finnish enlisted man named Jonas Kekola. He was whipped in public for a minor prank and wound up killing his Russian commanding officer by accident. He was imprisoned, escaped and became the most hunted man in Finland while becoming the hero of the Finnish people.

A series of raids and harassment by the followers of Jonas made a good start on a full-blown resistance movement.

Jonas was persuaded to go to America with his pregnant wife to preserve the emblem of freedom, mainly Jonas himself. His best friend, Vilho, took over from Jonas and behaved as though Jonas had never left.

This, then, is the continuing story of the fight for independence of the Finnish people.

Chapter One

Crazy Jake

This incident occurred in the town of Kiivijarvi in mid-Finland. It started a series of events that made Vilho Maki a formidable leader for the resistance movement against the oppressive Russian yoke.

*   *   *   *   *

Jake wasn't really crazy in the true sense of the word. He had problems that didn't quite allow him to conform to the rest of the world. His idea of correct social behavior was inconsistent with everyone else's.

Jake was tall, rawboned, with sandy red hair and sparkling blue eyes. Most of the time he wore an impish grin for all the world to see that he was happy.

While he was strong, his body tended slightly to obesity. This look deceived the average onlooker about the strength contained in that uncaring package of humanity.

People did tease him. Those that knew him limited the teasing to his body. He got mad when teased about his intelligence and his freckles.

Someone once told him he got his freckles by standing too close behind a cow. He hadn't liked that. His real sensitivity came when someone called him dumb.

A horse kicked Jake in the head when he was young. By all rights it should have killed him, but he did survive with some mental problems. The impairment of his mental faculties hardly affected his zest for life or his happy-go-lucky attitude. The worries in his life consisted of a place to sleep, his cat, something to eat and occasionally enough money to go on a drinking spree.

John Maki provided him a place to sleep in his horse barn. The barn was small as John kept a team of work horses there to do custom hauling. Jake slept in the loft in the summer and down with the horses when it got cold. The horses kept the barn warm. Jake preferred the loft, staying up there until late in the fall and going back up in early spring.

Everyone noticed the strong stable smell along with Jake's heavy body odor. Jake wasn't one for frequent bathing. People learned to stay upwind of him as much as possible. T h e y treated Jake well despite his stench and his mental problems. In all respects, he was a child except in body. Most of the teasing Jake received was in fun, and Jake went along with it. Most of the time Jake didn't know he was the butt of a joke. He laughed with everyone else, not knowing why they were laughing.

Once, though, some locals pushed him too far. The results were devastating. The ensuing skirmish let everyone know Jake's point of no return. The time to back off was when Jake quit smiling and started frowning.

The one time they pushed him too far, he nearly wrecked the place. He got his hands on two of his tormentors and would have killed them, but the bartender laid him low with a mallet.

The next morning Jake was all contrite and apologetic. It took him three years to pay for damage done in fifteen minutes.

The next incident occurred at the Boar's Head Tavern. Jake became fond of Mika, the owner, who always treated him with respect. It was one of Jake's periodic sprees. Normally, his sprees didn't amount to much as he soon ran out of money. This time he'd been working steady, cutting timber. The man for whom he was cutting feared that, if he paid him, he wouldn't come back for a week or so until all the money was gone. He held most of it until all the timber was cut. The extra money allowed Jake to continue his spree a bit longer.

Jake made good money. He was a good logger and a hard worker. He rarely had extra money as he was too generous with it. He gave some of it away but mostly he spent it buying drinks for his so-called friends. When the money ran out so did most of his friends, but Jake didn't notice or else didn't care. He was out for a good time.

So, on the night of his big spree, he had some extra money and was spending it freely. Several, so-called friends were there, soaking up drinks at Jake's expense. They were patting him on the back and commenting on his strength. Jake basked in all the attention.

"You're a good man Jake. We really like you."

"Well, I like you men, too, all of you. Have another drink on me."

"Thanks we will. Hey, bartender, another round on Jake!"

So it went. Jake knew vaguely that they were taking him, but he didn't care. He continued to luxuriate in the limelight of the men around him. Like an affection-starved puppy, he soaked up attention.

Ignorance wasn't a good excuse for the Russian officers to use about Jake. The locals had warned them about pushing Jake too far. The local people had told the Russians about Jake's early warning signs. When his laughter turned to a frown, all hell was going to break loose.

The six Russian officers stopped by the Boar's Head Tavern for drinks. Plainly, they'd been drinking elsewhere as they were a little tipsy and boisterous. They saw the locals getting drinks on Jake and thought that and sport at Jake's expense a great idea. They moved their table close, which rankled the locals.

Jake ignored the officers' kidding, or maybe he didn't realize he was the butt of their jokes. The Russians were crude and obtuse in the jokes they were playing on Jake.

Jake offered to buy his friends another drink. One of the Russians asked, "What's the matter, do you not like Russians? How come you don't buy us a drink?"

Jake stammered, "You . . . you're right. I don't like Russkies, and I'm not buying you any drinks!"

The comment went wrong with the Russians. The term "Russkie" was slightly derogatory. Their anger up, they started to tease Jake in earnest. "You dumb Finlander, you wouldn't make a good door mat for a Russian."

They all laughed, and Jake laughed with them until he saw his friends weren't laughing. A slight frown formed on his brow.

Mika said, "You people are getting Jake mad. When you see that frown forming instead of laughter, it's like a big thunderstorm. You better back off, Jake can get pretty mean."

"You think he could take all of us? We stick together, you know. I don't know if we could take out everyone in here, but we could give it a good try."

"We wouldn't interfere," said Mika. "We would just sit back and watch.

The Russians laughed and continued their harassment. Jake's laughter got quieter and his frown deeper.

"Jake, I suppose you're a friend of that outlaw Jonas that we've been chasing all over the country?"

This got Jake mad. Jonas was a true friend who always had treated Jake kindly whether drunk or sober.

"You bet Jonas is a friend of mine . . . a real friend. I like him a lot. He's no outlaw. You Russkies made him that way."

"He's a common criminal running around in the woods. A wild animal. We'll hunt him down like any other animal gone mad."

"He's n-n-not a criminal or a-a animal," stammered Jake.

Jake stammered more as he got madder. When he stopped talking it was best to get clear or get caught in the melee that certainly would follow.

"Jonas is s-s-sm-smart. You Russkies have chased him a long time and haven't caught him."

"Ah, he has dumb luck, we'll catch him and kill him."

"He's n-n-not dumb. Maybe I'm d-d-dumb, but Jonas is s-s-sm-smart."

Jake didn't like the word dumb. Too often it came with a derogatory statement describing himself.

The Russians had found his soft spot. Those that did not understand Finnish were told by the several that could to chant in unison.

"Dumb, you are dumb, dumb, dumb."

Jake toyed with his glass, making wet circles on the table, not looking at the Russians, his frown very deep.

"Dummy," one Russian said, pushing at Jake's shoulder, "What can you do about it? Dummy."

"I could do a lot, but Mika won't let me to fight in his place."

"You don't know how to fight. None of you Finns know how to fight."

"Oh, I know how to fight all right," said Jake slowly, "I just don't like to fight anymore. I break things up and hurt people."

The Russians took this as a sign of cowardice and pushed harder. "You're too yellow to fight. You're just a big dumb ox. You and your friend Jonas are both yellow. Jonas always runs away. He won't stay and fight."

This was too much, slandering the name of his best friend. A fist exploded in the face of the young, pimply-faced Russian officer who made the last remark. It broke his nose and took three teeth with it. One down, five to go.

The locals quickly moved away. Jake would hit anyone close when he was mad.

The Russians moved in to avenge their comrade. That was a big mistake. If they had left well enough alone, it might have ended then and there.

While there were five of them left, no two could match Jake in weight or strength under normal conditions. In his enraged state there was no contest.

Jake was still sitting when the next one got close. Jake kicked him in the knee. As he fell Jake helped him down by grabbing the back of his head and slamming his face into the table. He was through. Jake stood up.

Mika wanted to stop the fight to protect his property but so far all Jake had broken was Russian bones. Mika felt the Russians had it coming so he sat back and watched.

A third Russian jumped in, and Jake clamped one of his huge hands around this man's throat hitting him full in the face with the other. The impact of his big fist against the Russian's face sounded like a sledge hammer hitting a watermelon. It even looked the same; red spurted everywhere from the man's mouth and nose. Jake held onto him momentarily until his realized that the man was out on his feet. The only thing keeping him erect was Jake's ham-like hand around his throat. Jake let go, and the man crumpled. Three down, three to go.

Number four moved in. Jake swept him into his arms with a giant bear hug. He literally squeezed the breath out of him. The two remaining Russians jumped him from both sides, hammering him with their fists. Jake was oblivious to their blows. He squeezed harder until the man went limp. Jake opened his arms to let him slither to the floor.

Jake stepped back one step and grabbed the two remaining Russians by the nape of their necks and slammed their heads together. They were through, but Jake wasn't sure. He put each of them in a hammer lock and slammed their heads alternately into a nearby post. With the second slam Jake knew they were done. Jake turned them loose and watched them collapse into heaps on the floor.

Jake dusted off his hands as if to say a job well done, which indeed, it was. The locals and Mika applauded. Jake beamed under the limelight.

"See Mika," he said, "this time I didn't break up any of your furniture."

Mika said, "I know, Jake, but I still don't like you fighting. You don't know what you're doing when you fight."

Jake hung his head contritely, "I'm sorry, Mika. I shouldn't have done it, but they made me mad about Jonas . . . and besides it was fun."

"All right, Jake, let me buy you a drink this time. That was a good job you did on those smart alecs."

Mika poured him a half tumbler of the fiery aquavit Scandinavian liquor. Jake's inside lip had a bad cut where one of the Russians landed a lucky punch. Jake downed the drink. Tears came to his eyes as the alcohol burned the raw cut in his mouth.

He blew out, saying, "Whew that hurts worse than when he hit me."

Everyone laughed including Jake.

Slowly, the Russians came back to some semblance of life. Each, looked around, groggily wondering what had happened and were very wary in case there was more of the same coming. They helped each other up to leave the premises.

As they left, one of them said, "You haven't heard the last of this, you damn dumb Finlander."

Jake made one step toward the door to hasten their exit. They hurried out.

Indeed, that wasn't the last of it, but, for the time being, Jake basked in the glory of a hero, and he loved it.

Two weeks later to the day, a group of Russians jumped Jake, stabbed and beat him then left him for dead.

They jumped Jake on his way home from the Boar's Head. Vilho, Jonas' close friend, found him alive but just barely. Vilho held him in his arms as he haltingly related what had happened to him.

"A bunch of Russkies jumped me . . . don't know how many. They had clubs and knives. I hurt them some, but they got me. Tell everyone goodbye. Take care of my cat over in the stable. He's a lot like me . . . he doesn't need much, just a little food and attention."

"Don't worry Jake. We'll take care of your cat, and I'll find out who did this to you. They will pay in kind."

With that Jake gave a slight shudder, his eyes glazed over, and he was gone. Vilho gently closed his eyes with his fingertips. Tears streamed down Vilho's face for the senseless loss of this simple man.

There were several trails of blood leading away from the scene. Jake had definitely inflicted damage on some of the group.

The people preparing Jake for burial found both arms broken, his nose and skull fractured, many large contusions plus eight stab wounds. They couldn't figure out how he lived as long as he had.

Most of the town turned out for his funeral. Simple as he was, Jake had been well liked and kind of the town pet. Sentiment ran high against the Russians. They did not have proof as to who had killed Jake, but they were sure it was the ones Jake had fought in the tavern. The perpetrators of the crime may have been uneasy seeing such a large turnout for a supposed nobody.

This incident added to the growing list of grievances the Russians were perpetrating on the Finnish people. Still, they couldn't understand why the Finns were mad at them all the time. Jake's murder went a long way toward stirring up resentment and strenthening the resistance movement even more.

Chapter Two

Revenge for Jake

VILHO WAS REALLY BOTHERED BY WHAT the Russians did to his friend, Crazy Jake. Everything Vilho could discover about the murder pointed to the Russians who Jake had beaten up earlier. Many clues pointed in that direction, but he couldn't find out the names of the guilty ones.

It stayed on his mind for several weeks. Finally he went to the Boar's Head to see if he could glean any more information about the men who had provoked Jake into the fight.

"The Russians aren't saying anything about the matter," said Mika. "I heard rumors some officers were treated for injuries the night it happened.

"What do you know about those Russians officers. Anything?"

"Nothing, really, they weren't regulars. In fact, I never saw any of them before or since. The only one I can remember anything about is the real young one with the pimply face. I thought at the time he was too young to be an officer. He probably has parents with influence. He was scared out of his wits, but he went along with the others in baiting Jake. I really think he went along with them to prove he was one of the bunch."

Vilho said, "I've seen that one around. He's part of the group that came in to observe field operations."

Mika said, "I might recognize the big burly one with the handlebar mustache. He was the one really pushing it. He folded like a wet sack when Jake hit him. It tickled me so I could hardly keep from laughing out loud."

"Kind of keep your eyes and ears open for anything that might shed a little light on this. I'll do the same, but you have a better chance of hearing something with all the people coming in here."

"What would you do if you found out who did it?'

That was a question Vilho wasn't prepared to answer. "I don't know. I haven't gone that far in my thinking. It just makes me mad that nothing is being done about it. I feel sure the Russians know who was involved, but they're not about to admit that to any of us."

Mika was fast becoming a staunch ally of the resistance movement and a friend of Vilho. He said, "You're going to have to take me fishing some time. I hear you know some spots no one but you has fished."

"Any time you want to go, just let me know. I hear that you're quite a fisherman. I do know a few places where we might pick up a trout or two."

"How about this weekend? "

"Pick you up about six in the morning so we can get a good start. If the weather turns sour, at least, we'll get in a little fishing.

They talked on into the night about fishing, hunting, and their mutual love of the outdoors. Both voiced concern about the future of freedom for Finland. They liked each other and were looking forward to the coming fishing trip.

Vilho went home thinking about the strange turn of events that brought him and Mika together. Crazy Jake's death might wind up having some meaning after all. Normally Vilho hardly gave Mika a second thought. Now, they were both involved in finding Jake's killers. Vilho vowed he would find them.

The next day Vilho found an excuse to go into the newly built transient officers' area. This was where he thought he had seen the pimply-faced young officer. He hid in one of the new buildings where he could see the officers' mess hall. No course of action came to mind if he did locate the man. It was near noon. If they are all going to be in one place, it would be here.

A group came in with a young lieutenant fitting the description Mika had given him. The other officers were teasing him unmercifully. He was taking it pretty well. For the time being, that was as much as Vilho wanted to know. The officer was here. He could find out who he was and some of his habits from the people working in the area.

"Why am I being so secretive about all this? I could just ask who he is and let it go," he said to himself.

He let the matter drop from his mind. He didn't want to examine his motives any closer.

The next day he found out the young officer's name was Pribiloff and that he had come from a powerful family. That accounted for his youthfulness as an officer. He was on detached duty along with some other officers. All of them were here to study field conditions and how to set up and run a frontier outpost. The officers would leave to set up similar outposts in other areas. The hunt for Jonas added spice to the operation.

On Saturday morning Vilho picked up Mika to go on their fishing trip. The weather looked fair with a few clouds. They were looking forward to a successful trip.

Mika was a little out of shape in comparison to Vilho. They had to stop often to let Mika catch his breath. It took them two hours of steady hiking to reach their destination, a series of small springs that fed into Rock Creek. This was the reason few, if any, knew the fishing spot.

The first spring was the largest with a grassy area set several feet above the bank of the spring hole. This was where they decided they would set up camp. Both men were anxious to get on with the fishing, so they just piled their gear in a heap on the bank. They both fished the first pond and both caught several trout.

Mika called across the pond, "At least we'll have enough for our supper tonight even if we don't catch anymore."

"Oh, we'll catch some more," Vilho assured him. "The spring holes down below will yield some big ones."

"I'm happy with this," Mika shouted back.

Vilho said, "Looks like rain. Do you want to go back into town or stick it out here?"

Mika replied, "Go back? Hell, no! I seldom get a chance to get out for fishing. I would as soon stick it out."

Their chosen camp site was a small, grassy plateau surrounded by spruce trees. Vilho gathered some rocks to make a fire place while Mika went to gather spruce boughs for their bed.

On Mika's second trip for boughs, he called, "Vilho, come over here and look at this."

Vilho straightened up from his rock gathering to saunter over to where Mika was standing,

"What is it?"

"It looks like a cave amongst the rocks."

It was getting a little dark, so Vilho made a torch to see better. The light indeed revealed a small cave.

Mika said, "Be careful, there may be an animal of some kind in there."

"No, there's no sign of animals going in or out. If they did use it, it was a long time ago."

Mika went into the cave saying, "We have a cozy spot to spend the night. We can build a fire at the entrance and be snug in here."

"Looks good to me," replied Vilho.

Vilho moved his fireplace rocks to the entrance while Mika finished gathering spruce boughs for their bed.

Mika cooked the trout over the open fire, and it was superb.

Vilho sat back after a wonderful meal and said, "Mika, that was the best trout I've ever eaten."

Mika said, "Wait until we get back to my place where I can really do it justice."

Vilho said, "This would make a good hideout if you ever needed one. I wonder if Jonas knew about this place?"

"I wonder how he's doing in America?"

"I don't know, but I expect to hear from him any day."

The talk drifted from Jonas to Jake and what Vilho found out so far on the Russians.

"Do you think you could get that young Pribiloff to talk if you got him alone?" asked Mika.

"Don't know for sure, but I'd like to try. I believe he's a little weak and would break with some . . . gentle persuasion."

Mika said, "I wouldn't want to experience your gentle persuasion."

"They weren't too gentle with Jake," said Vilho seriously, remembering Jake's battered body.

"I'm sorry. I know how much you liked Jake. So did I. I wish I could be of more help, but that's the only time they've been in my place. There's only three places they could go to get drunk. One is my place, two is Old Charlie's. The Russians have their own lounge, too. Quite a few Russians stop at Old Charlie's even though it's a dump. It's a lot closer to their quarters than my place."

Vilho said, "I guess I'm going to have to pay Old Charlie a visit when I get back."

"I haven't been here very long, but I know Old Charlie isn't going to tell you anything."

"Oh, I know, but I thought I might pick up something useful just hanging around the place."

The campfire burned down, Vilho got up and threw on some more wood. They both lay at the entrance to the cave watching the flickering embers of the fire, each man thinking his own private thoughts.

Mika said, "I'm getting a little sleepy. I think I'll turn in. I want to be up bright and early for the trout."

"Me too. I could use a little sleep myself."

With that, both men laid their bedrolls just inside the mouth of the cave.

It rained during the night. Vilho woke up to the thunder and lightning, glad that they were in the dry cave. The rain started with a few spattering drops but soon developed into a full downpour. Vilho watched the storm through the lightning flashes. The water dripped off the mouth of the cave to drown out the remnants of their fire. Mika slept soundly through it all.

Morning came, bright and clear. The rain had washed the skies clear, leaving everything looking like bright jewels. Vilho got up to scout for some dry wood. The down side of some fallen trees yielded a few dry pieces. The fire was going and breakfast half cooked when Mika woke.

"Get up, lazy bones," teased Vilho. "The day is half gone. The trout are jumping all over the place."

"Hey, I was planning on cooking breakfast."

"You have to get up early to do that. Besides I wanted to repay you for the superb trout last night,"

Breakfast over, Mika asked, "Vilho, have you come to a decision what to do if you find out which Russians killed Jake?"

"I keep thinking of everything I would do to those people. I would be like them if I killed them, though. I think I'll turn over any proof I find to the Russians. If they don't do anything, then I don't know what I'll do."

Mika snickered scornfully. "Vilho, you're an optimist if you think the Russians are going to do anything. One Finn that was not all there is nothing in comparison to Russian officers."

Vilho bristled and retorted, "Damn it. You're probably right, but I have to hope and try to believe they'll do what's right. If I can prove beyond a doubt their people did it, they might do something about it."

"Vilho, Vilho, my friend, you're sitting there lying to yourself. I'd like to see them do right, but it'll never happen. Those people don't understand public relations. If they actually did something about it, it would be a big step toward smoother

14

relations with us. Finns might think we could live together in harmony, but those Russians won't look at it that way."

"I know, and I'm not sure I can prove what happened to Jake to myself, let alone anyone else."

They packed up their gear and headed for the spring holes and more fish. They caught several fish to take home. Mika caught and released several more.

Mika said, "I hate to go back. This has been a superb fishing trip. I appreciate your bringing me here. Anything I can do for you in the future, just let me know. I've really enjoyed your company, and I do share your views on freedom. I don't share your views on the Russians doing anything about Jake's murder, though."

The trip back to town went quickly. Mika was tired but happy. As they parted company, he said, "Come by tomorrow night about supper time. I'll have that trout fixed for you like you would not believe."

"Right now I should go to Charlie's place and see if I can find out anything about those Russian officers. I hate to fish and run, but Jake's killers are still unpunished, and it's kind of bothering me."

"Kind of? I'd appreciate anything you find out."

* * * * *

Vilho sat at a table by himself, noting the difference between Old Charlie's Place and Mika's. He couldn't understand why anyone would frequent the run-down place if he had a choice. Old Charlie's smelled of decaying wood, stale beer, tobacco smoke, and assorted greasy cooking odors. The tables looked as if they hadn't been washed in a month. The floor looked as if it hadn't been swept, let alone scrubbed, since the place was built. Mika's place, by comparison, was always neat and clean.

Charlie was about the same caliber as his place. He had a two-day growth of beard, and his once-white apron showed the signs of all the meals he cooked in the past week. His clothes looked and smelled as if he had slept in them. More than likely he had.

Vilho nursed his second warm beer, idly making wet circles in the dirt on the table. Pribiloff and his group came in. They were loud and boisterous. Vilho assumed they had been drinking at the officers' lounge.

Vilho looked them over and wondered just what the attraction was in this place versus their own lounge. He had been in their lounge, and it was very plush. Maybe senior officers would frown on their boisterous conduct.

The group was picking on Pribiloff. This time he was not taking it as well as before. They were teasing him about some woman with whom he either had had a date or was thinking of asking for a date. Vilho couldn't tell which.

Vilho's understanding of Russian was not sufficient to tell for sure what the men were saying, but he could see that Pribiloff was getting madder by the minute. The madder he got, the more the group teased him. Shortly, Pribiloff got up, practically in tears, said something to the group and headed for the door. The group threw more comments after him as he left.

Vilho waited a few minutes, then followed. No one took notice of his leaving. Charlie was in back, and the Russians were laughing and joking, apparently about Pribiloff. Vilho followed the young officer for some distance before he realized the folly of his actions.

"What am I doing? I can't speak Russian, and I doubt if he speaks any Finn. How am I going to question him about the incident?"

He headed back to the Boar's Head.

As soon as he sat down, Mika asked him if he had found out anything. Vilho explained his dilemma, not able to question the young Pribiloff.

Mika shrugged. "Look, I can translate for you. I learned Russian a long time ago when I had the place in Helsinki."

Vilho declined the offer with a shake of his head. "Mika, I don't want you to get involved in this. This is my problem."

"It's my problem too. If you don't get involved in freedom personally then you don't deserve to be free."

It was a good point. "All right. If you're sure. I don't know where he was going. Maybe I should have followed him further. He wasn't heading back to their quarters."

"I know where he was going. I heard some rumors about a young Russian officer romancing the young Keski widow."

The two of them left to see if they could catch Pribiloff when he came away from his love tryst.

They walked up near the Keski house to stand in the shadows. The house was dark.

Vilho whispered, "Looks like we missed him."

Mike shook his head. "No, I don't think so. Let's wait awhile. We don't have anything else to do anyway."

They stood and shifted from one foot to another, fidgeted, talked in low tones until some lights came on in the house.

Mika smiled. "See, I told you to wait awhile. I believe he's in there. I just saw two shadows against the window shade."

They didn't have long to wait before the door opened, casting a long oblong of yellow light followed by a shadow and Pribiloff himself.

As Pribiloff came by their shadowy hiding place, they stepped out and grabbed him by both arms. Even in the dim light, they could see him blanch white in fear. He babbled something in Russian, and Mika spoke to him. All Vilho could do was listen and collect a word or two. Mika and Pribiloff talked back and forth, with the conversation becoming more animated. He could tell that Pribiloff was giving Mika some names.

Mika gave Pribiloff a push and took Vilho by the arm, rapidly walking away until they were out of earshot.

Mika said, "I didn't speak to you in Finn on purpose. I acted like I was another Russian investigating the incident. I swore him to secrecy after I got the information out of him. He and the others really did kill Jake because of the fight in my place. He swore he only watched as the others beat Jake. A Captain Malenkov was the ring leader. He's the one with the big moustache. The other four are lieutenants Karkov, Gorki, Ivanov, and Karchov."

"I'll remember those names for sure," said Vilho, "I would like to take them all on tonight."

Mika said, "I'll go with you, if you want. There's only five of them. If we take them by surprise, it'll be no contest."

Vilho considered. "No. First I'm going to send a letter to the commandant and see if they do anything. I doubt they will, but I'll give them that chance first."

Mike patted his shoulder. "You're a dreamer but go ahead."

"If they do nothing, then I'll get them. If I can, I'll take my time about it so the ones left will wonder who's next. I want them to know they can't get away with killing a Finn."

They arrived back at Mika's to discover that the culprits in question had left Old Charlie's and were there. Vilho seethed in anger and had a hard time holding back.

Mika kept an eye on him and said calmly and quietly, "Slow down, Vilho. You don't want to give yourself away so soon. You said in your own sweet time, *if* the Russians do nothing. At least Pribiloff didn't run right to them and tattle. He must have gone straight home, quaking in his boots. For the time being, we're safe from him spilling everything."

Vilho relaxed visibly. Mika ordered some wine sent to his table. Vilho gulped it down, ordering another, slowly relaxing while his brain raced, formulating and discarding plans for revenge on the Russians.

He said to himself. "I probably should have killed Pribiloff even with Mika present."

Vilho made up his mind that if he did decide to kill them, Malenkov would be the last to go. He wanted him to fear for his life.

No precise plan would come to mind. Some way the culprits would have to know death was coming. At least they would be helpless to do anything about it. The Russians needed to know that this kind of deed would bring reprisals from the Finnish people.

Vilho was so intent on his thoughts for revenge that he forgot about his original plan—notify Russian headquarters that these men had killed a Finnish national in cold blood. He felt it was an exercise in futility, but he was going to go through the motions anyway.

The next morning Vilho dropped a letter off in the commandant's office. Mika wrote the note in Russian, stating the facts and asking that justice be done.

A clerk in Rykov's office told Vilho there was a perfunctory hearing, and the men involved denied any knowledge. Everyone laughed, saying it was some kind of crank letter.

Vilho made up his mind right then. "I'm going to avenge Jake's death to show the Russians," he said through clenched teeth.

That evening he returned to the Boar's Head to see if the culprits would show up there again.

Vilho said to Mika, "I'll go back to Charlie's if they don't show up soon, but that place really gets me down."

"It would get me down, too."

"I've been thinking of some way to let those Russkies know I'm going to kill them because of what they did to Crazy Jake."

Mike nodded. "I know you want them to know it's a Finn killing them in revenge. We'd be better off making them guess if it's one of us or another Russian. Is killing them really what you have in mind?"

Vilho nodded firmly. "Yes, I want to kill them. Why would we want to have them think it might be another Russian?"

"If they know for sure it was a Finn doing the killing, they might do some reprisals on our countrymen."

That was a good point. "I see what you mean."

"How about we pretend it was Jonas in some way? They never made reprisals on anything he did. It'd go a long way in perpetuating the legend of Jonas even though he's not here."

"I've been thinking about how we could get recognition for our resistance group. We could use a cloth emblem or something symbolizing a ghost because that's what they called

Jonas several times after he had disappeared into thin air practially under their noses."

"The first time we could leave a note explaining that this was the Ghost. After that, all we'd have to do is leave the emblem."

The idea sat well with Vilho. "This deed with the Russians and Crazy Jake would be a good motive to start."

They were still talking when the Russian officers came in. Malenkov and Pribiloff were missing.

Vilho said, "It's good they break up at times. I was wondering how I could separate them or get them in smaller groups. I wonder where Malenkov and Pribiloff are tonight?"

"I would venture to guess that Pribiloff is with the Keski widow again. I'll try to eavesdrop on the group and see if I can find out more about Malenkov. They don't know I know Russian."

The Russians started waving madly for service, so Mika walked over. They kept telling him what they wanted, and Mika acted as if he didn't understand. It irked Mika that Russians refused to learn Finnish unless ordered to do so by their commanding officers. Mika finally acted as if he understood. When he brought their orders back to the table, he pantomimed asking where Malenkov was by showing the bigness and the big moustache. He got the answer back in pantomime that he was with a woman and would join them later.

Mika reported to Vilho, "Malenkov is with a woman and will be in later. If we don't find out who he's with tonight, you may have to follow him to see where he goes."

Malenkov did come in later, but Mika could glean no more information as to the woman he was seeing. The others did tease him about an older woman, though, and Malenkov laughingly made the remark about older women really being appreciative of attention.

"I haven't heard of any one fraternizing with the Russians lately. I have no idea who it could be," said Vilho.

Closing time came, Mika shooed the Russians out the door, with them objecting all the way.

Mika and Vilho sat down together, drinking a little more wine while his help cleaned up. Mika was restless, jumping up every few minutes to do some little chore. He was too impatient to wait for the help to do it.

Vilho said, "I'm going to go, too. I'll get in touch as soon as I hear from Jonas."

"Come back tomorrow night. It gets lonesome around here."

"I better not, I might do something rash to those Russkies. I need to wait for the right opportunity."

Vilho headed for the door. Before he walked completely out, Mika asked, "What about Malenkov's girlfriend?"

"I'll have to think about that," replied Vilho as he went out the door.

Walking home, Vilho kept thinking how to use the ghost symbol in his revenge plans on the Russians. The next night Vilho did return to Mika's tavern, but he came early so he could talk about using the ghost symbol.

Vilho said. "I think we should use the ghost symbol to keep the image of Jonas, the Ghost, alive. That could have benefits."

Mika replied, "I think you're right. I think we can do a lot with the Jonas ghost symbol. We can use my place as a clearing house for the group. No one would think twice about anyone coming in and out of here . . . even late. I have another piece of good news for you. Malenkov is spending evenings at the Kovala house. He's courting their oldest daughter. They've been trying to get her married off for years. I guess they're desperate enough to push her off on anybody, even a Russian."

"Mika, thanks. I need one more favor, though. Write a note in Russian stating that Jonas, the Ghost, is avenging the death of Crazy Jake. I'm going to leave it on the body of the first Russian murderer I kill, along with one of the ghost emblems. The rest of them can worry about when their time is coming.

"Right now, the only ones I'll get alone are Pribiloff and Malenkov. The others stick together in a group all the time. I believe I can take any two of them, but I doubt I can get four unless I shoot them. I would rather get them one at a time. I want to give others time to worry and wonder and get really afraid," said Vilho.

Mika said, "The minute you kill the first one, the rest are going to be on the alert. It's going to be a lot harder to get to the rest."

"I know. I've given it a lot of thought. If I can get them when they think they're safe, it'll be better. The rest of the Russkies will know they can't get away with killing a Finn."

"Sounds good," said Mika, "If you need any help let me know."

Vilho smiled at the sincerity in Mika's face. "You've been a lot of help already, but killing isn't in your line of work."

"It could be in this case. I really liked Jake. The fight wasn't a big enough reason to kill a man."

"Just write me that note. Hard to tell when my first opportunity will come up."

Mika went into the back and came out with the note in Russian. He said, "I hope you get this over with soon so we can get in some more fishing."

The four officers—Karkov, Gorki, Ivanov and Karchov—came in. They were in their usual drunken, boisterous condition. Immediately they shouted orders in Russian to Mika. Mika strolled over slowly, acting extra stupid to annoy them.

Mika winked at Vilho as he went by with their order after much effort on the Russian's part. When he returned with their drinks, Mika acted clumsy and dumped a schooner of beer into the Ivanov's lap. The officer jumped up, cursing and angry enough that he might hit Mika. Mika was all apologetic and contrite, so Ivanov let it go. Ivanov announced he was going back to get a dry uniform and would be back as soon as he could.

Mika came by Vilho's table and quietly informed him that Ivanov was going back to change. Vilho reacted quickly and made it out the door a few minutes before Ivanov. Hiding in the shadows, he waited. When the man emerged, Vilho followed at a discreet distance. The route was familiar. Mentally, he ran through the places to waylay the man. The best choice lay ahead, but he couldn't think of a way to get ahead of him.

Then the thought came to him. "I'll wait until he's on his way back. That way our leaving so close together will not be so suspicious."

Vilho slowed his pace to let Ivanov get ahead, leaving less chance for discovery. When he came to the place he had in mind, he stopped, slid quietly into the shadows to await the return of Ivanov. He didn't have long to wait. A little while later, Ivanov came hurredly down the road. Vilho stepped out of the shadows and faced him. Mika taught Vilho the one Russian sentence he wanted to use at this moment.

In his best Russian, Vilho said, "This is for killing a good Finn that did nothing to you except have a bar room fight."

Ivanov gasped for breath as he tried to get away. Vilho's knife caught him as he turned. Ivanov's next gasp for breath was his last. Vilho pulled his knife free and wiped it on the falling Ivanov. When he was down, Vilho rolled the note and stuck it in his mouth. He put the ghost symbol in his hand and closed his fingers so it wouldn't get lost.

Vilho looked at Ivanov and said under his breath, "One down, five more to go."

* * * * *

The other three officers waited in vain for Ivanov to return. Closing time came, and Mika pushed the three of them out the door.

Mika said to himself, "I wonder if Vilho caught up to Ivanov?"

The three officers were wending their drunken way home when they stumbled on the body of Ivanov. At first they thought he was drunk and had passed out until Gorki reached down to revive him. He was aghast as his hand came away, dripping with blood. It scared everyone in the group. They all started looking around nervously. After a short conference, they decided higher authorities should handle the problem.

Everyone sobered up quickly as they hurried back to head-quarters. The night officer didn't believe their story at first. Gorki convinced him by showing the blood on his hand.

The night officer sent a messenger to wake the medics to retrieve the body. Major Rykov was wakened and informed. Rykov, a major from Helsinki, had come to Kiivijarvi to personally supervise the search for the rebel, Jonas. He was raving mad at being awakened and lashed out at anyone close.

At the dispensary the note in Ivanov's mouth was discovered, as was the ghost symbol clenched in his fist.

When Rykov heard about it, he grew livid with rage, screaming, "One damn Finn is still outwitting this whole damn detachment. I need someone with competence to deal with this simple problem. I can't do it all myself!"

Everyone who could ease out of his office headed for cover. The unfortunate remaining few caught the brunt of his wrath.

"In the morning I want every available patrol out looking for Jonas. He can't have gone far in the night. No, rescind that order! Split the group and search the town from one end to the other and through every house while the other half searches the woods. He's not a cat, he can't see at night. I am sure he's not far away."

A comment from outside the window floated in, "He might not be a cat but he sure as hell acts like a ghost."

"Who said that?" screamed Rykov out the window, trying to get past the screen so he could see. Everyone outside scattered like a covey of quail.

The next two days' search was in vain. It aggravated the townspeople and little else. The other half of the search produced only tired men and more tired horses.

Vilho kept a low profile while the search was in progress. When it cooled down a little, he went back to the Boar's Head to see Mika.

Mika greeted him quietly with an under-the-breath question, "Did you get the job done or was it someone else? I didn't hear about any note or ghost symbol."

"It was me, but they're keeping it all hush hush. They're all embarrassed about the whole episode," said Vilho grinning.

"The word will leak out about the note and symbol. Just wait. When that happens, everyone will have a big laugh about the dumb Russkies."

The officers, including Malenkov, kept close to their compound. Vilho learned that young Pribiloff had requested immediate return to Russia. The request was granted because of the importance of his father in Nicholas II's court.

Vilho said to Mika when he heard, "I wasn't keen on killing Pribiloff anyway. I believe he was telling the truth when he said he just watched."

Mika said, "Those officers are keeping a low profile since the demise of Ivanov. I heard that Olga Kovala has been writing impassioned pleas to Malenkov to visit her. He's written her notes but still hasn't left the compound. He'll break soon."

Vilho nodded, then smiled and said, "Our ruse did work, though. They've been looking for Jonas like crazy. All they really accomplished was get more people mad at them. We picked up a few more for the resistance movement. Some are mad at the Russians for the highhanded search. Others came believing in our cause and that we can win."

Vilho and Mika talked on into the night hoping the Russian officers might show. Vilho walked down to Old Charlie's and back to see if they had showed up there but no luck.

Vilho said, "I didn't go into Old Charlie's, I just looked through the window. I can't stand that dump."

They parted company that night, and Vilho kept checking to see if any of the rabbits had come out of the warren but no luck. Two weeks went by, and Vilho made up his mind he was going to have to go into the compound and ferret them out. The big question was how to do it?

After much thought about one plan and another Vilho came up with one he thought workable.

Through friends of his in headquarters, he found out the room numbers of the men he wanted. Gorki and Karkov roomed together, Karchov roomed with another man by the name of Romanoff. Malenkov had his own room in the same building.

Several nights of discreet observation told Vilho the routine at the officers' quarters. Two of the guards he could avoid by going around their routine patrols. The third guard would have to be neutralized some way so he could gain entrance to the building. He guarded the door. Vilho chose the quick way. He avoided the patrolling guards and hit the door guard on the head. He bound and gagged him then dragged him behind some stacked lumber. He knew he could get away with one round of the patrolling guards as the door guard went inside at times.

Vilho's pulse quickened as he moved down the hall to where Gorki and Karkov roomed. The hall was dimly lit, so he had to get close to each door to see the numbers.

Until that moment, he had not thought about the possibility of locked doors. He gently tried their door, and much to his relief, the door opened easily. Stepping inside, he stood by the door, barely breathing while he became accustomed to the darkened room. Heavy snoring came from one bed while a slight wheezing whistle came from the other. He wasn't sure which one was which but they both had to go. He decided on the wheezer first as the abrupt stopping of snoring might rouse the other one.

He moved in as the wheezer turned, mumbling in his sleep. Vilho stood stock still barely breathing himself. The wheezer's nasal whistle resumed. Vilho discerned he was lying on his side with his back to him. A quick knife thrust into the kidney stopped the wheezing. The kidney thrust is so painful that the victim will not utter a sound. Vilho then dropped one of the ghost symbols on the bed.

Next, he moved across the room to wipe his razor sharp blade across the upturned throat of the snoring man. The snoring turned into a gurgle, and Vilho knew he was gone. He dropped another symbol.

He slipped down the hall to the Karchov-Romanoff room. He knew Karchov occupied the bed on the left side of the room. Karchov had his back to him, so Vilho gave him the kidney thrust and dropped another symbol. As he turned to leave, he kicked a boot, and it clattered against the bed. Romanoff stirred and, for a minute, Vilho thought he was going to have to kill him, but the steady breathing resumed.

He proceeded down the hall to Malenkov's room, disappointed to find it empty. Vilho walked out the door. He paused long enough to see if the guard was all right. The guard groaned as he went by, so Vilho just walked away. He felt sure there would be no investigation until morning even though the guard was slugged, bound and gagged.

Vilho walked home. He wanted to talk to Mika, but he knew he was in bed a long time hence. He didn't want to wake him.

He thought as he walked. "Four away, one to go. Pribiloff didn't really count. I'm disappointed Malenkov was not in his room. He may be back to seeing Olga again. Hell, I ought to check on him. Maybe I could get it all done tonight!"

He turned on his heel to head for the Kovala house. As late as it was, lights shown from the living room windows. John Kovala was strict about keeping lights on when men friends visited his daughter even though he wanted her to get married.

Vilho slipped close enough to discern that, indeed, Malenkov sat in the house.

"I can wait for you, captain," Vilho said to himself, "just like you must have waited for poor Jake."

He knew the exact route Malenkov would have to take back to the compound. A deserted spot in the road concealed by a clump of trees became his hiding place. With his knife, he cut a big, heavy stick from one of the saplings in the clump. Ready, he hunkered down and watched the road. He didn't have long to wait. As he suspected, old man Kovala would not let Malenkov stay very late.

The big, hulking, figure of Malenkov came down the road. Vilho stepped into the road, giving him the same sentence in

Russian that he had given Ivanov. Vilho recognized the cursing in Russian but nothing else as Malenkov charged him like an enraged bull, head down and roaring. The first swing of Vilho's stick caught him in the right knee and sent him spinning to the ground. He tried to get up but his knee wouldn't respond. Vilho got methodical. He broke both his arms, then the other knee as the man tried to get up again. By this time, Malenkov was sobbing and pleading for his life in Russian and Finnish. Vilho stopped the pleading with a vicious swing to the mouth. He was out, but Vilho put his knife into him before he threw down the last of the ghost symbols.

The next day, the search for Jonas intensified. Every able-bodied Russian was in on it. Jonas, in America, was oblivious of the whole event, of course. As it happened, at that very moment, he and Emma were fishing a new stream in Michigan and thoroughly enjoying themselves, though Vilho knew Jonas would have enjoyed it even more, knowing what was happening in town.

That night Vilho saw Mika and said, "It's done. Never ask me about any of the details. It's done. That's all."

Mika squeezed his arm and went to get him a bottle of wine.

Chapter Three

Revenge Reaction

ROMANZOF WOKE UP, STRETCHED and looked over at his sleeping roommate. Usually Karchov was an early riser. Romanzof wondered idly what was keeping him abed so late. He called over to him, "What's the matter Karchov? Did you sneak out for some fun and games last night after I went to sleep?"

No reply.

"Come on, lazy. I was relying on you to wake me up like always. We're going to be late."

Romanzof went over to shake him. He recoiled when his hand touched the stiff body. There was a small streak of dry blood on the covers from the kidney wound, most of the bleeding having occurred internally. He wasn't sure he was dead until he turned him over. Dull, lifeless eyes stared back at him. Romanzof stood, stunned for a moment, then ran down the hall in his underwear screaming, "Karchov is dead, murdered, dead!"

Heads popped out of every room to see what the noise was about. The only doors remaining closed were those to the Gorki-Karkov room and Malenkov's. Silence reigned for a minute while everyone looked at each other and the still closed doors of the hall. One of the men closest to the Gorki-Karkov room gathered enough courage to open the door and peek inside. He came out retching violently. When he got his breath he said, "They're both dead. What's going on in this place?"

Another officer took a quick look in Malenkov's room and announced almost with relief that it was empty.

Almost everyone was sick from the retching and the realization that three of their friends had been murdered. Everyone took it for granted that the men were dead. No one wanted to go in and make sure.

Romanzof, still incoherent, saw one of the other officers dressed and screamed at him, "Don't just stand there, go get Gerchenoff!"

The shouting snapped everyone out of their daze. They all went back into their rooms to dress. All the doors stayed open and conversations were extra loud.

By the time Gerchenoff arrived, everyone was dressed and milling around.

Captain Gerchenoff, the new commander of the post's day-to-day operations, had been promoted to the job when his commander was killed by Jonas.

He came from the court of Czar Nicholas for an indiscretion involving him and the paramour of a high ranking court officer. He was transferred to this far flung outpost as punishment.

He had been trim and neat when he was a member of the elite palace guard, but in Kiivijarvi he had let his body go to fat. He was sloppy in attire. He drank too much, and it showed in the small red spider veins in his face. His eyes, while brown, were always bleary and bloodshot. He was rarely seen before ten in the morning, and then he often had a bad hangover from the previous night's drinking.

Gerchenoff wasn't a happy commander. He had lots of problems thrust upon him. The main one being his command's inability to catch Jonas. The Finns hindered his command intensely.

Gerchenoff had been an easy-going officer, taking orders readily from those above him and rarely having to make any major decisions himself. As post commander, however, he had to make them, and it seemed everything he did was wrong.

Rykov was an irritating thorn in Gerchenoff's side. He constantly berated him for failing to catch Jonas. Rykov bragged when he left Helsinki that he, personally, would have the man in irons in two weeks. Now almost a year had gone by, and they were still no closer to catching him.

There was no way they would catch Jonas as he and his wife, Emma, and the new baby were safe in America but the Russians didn't know that.

"Did anyone see or hear anything during the night?" asked Gerchenoff, ashen faced, after he viewed the bodies. "What about you, Romanzof, you were in the same room with Karchov?"

"I didn't see or hear a thing. I woke up to find him dead."

"All right, all right. Everyone clear the quarters. I'll make arrangements for getting the bodies out of here. Has anyone seen Malenkov?"

One of the officers volunteered, "He went into town last night to visit his new girl friend. Probably stayed the night."

Over a solemn breakfast, word came in that Malenkov's battered body had been found with one of the ghost symbols lying beside it. Speculation flew about the possibility of emblems present with the other bodies.

They questioned Romanzof, "Did you see anything like that near Karchov?"

"Yes, come to think of it. I did see a little piece of rag or something with black spots. I thought it was something belonging to Karchov. He's such a messy person. I thought it was some rag he threw down."

Silence around the table became almost unbearable. Someone laughed nervously and said, "I'm glad it wasn't me, that's all."

Further investigation found the other ghost symbols in the Gorki-Karkov room. The bound guard was found.

The furor increased in tempo. Extra guards were posted all around. Everyone became suspicious of everyone else. Was it really Jonas, or was it one of their own, gone berserk? How could Jonas get past all the guards and then out again without anyone seeing him? The ghost theory grew. Some thought it was one of their own taking advantage of the situation to commit murder.

Gerchenoff suspected it was Jonas or one of his men. All the men killed were involved in the killing of Crazy Jake. The exception was Pribiloff who transferred back to Russia. The earlier killing of Ivanov with the note and ghost symbol pointed in that direction.

Gerchenoff called in Chekok and said, "I'm sending you to Helsinki with a dispatch for Golovin. I want you to persuade Golovin not to come up here. All I need is that fat, overbearing, tub of lard up here shouting orders. Golovin and that damn Rykov would be too much to take. I'll just go out and join Jonas in the bush or something."

Chekok was glad to go. He would get some respite from the monotony of Kiivijarvi.

He said, "Yes sir, but I doubt that I can convince Golovin not to come. These killings may be the last straw. He was talking about coming up, but Rykov talked him out of it. But, sir, if he did come, it would only be for a short while. He couldn't stand being away from Helsinki for very long."

Gerchenoff sighed. "Do what you can. Dismissed."

Chekok told the orderly to send someone to the stables to get his horse ready as he was leaving within the hour. He went back to his quarters, throwing clothes into his saddle bags. The orderly delivered his horse, and he was on his way to Helsinki in short order.

* * * * *

Vilho went to the Boar's Head to see Mika and get his mind off recent events. Mika's booming, jovial self, kidding him about everything, helped him forget. He suggested several items on the menu, but Vilho asked him to wait.

"I want to have a few drinks and relax before I think about food."

Mika came back with a bottle of wine and two glasses and shared a drink.

"I know you'll like this wine," Mika told him. "It's one of my favorites. I seldom sell any. I give it away once in a while to some of my special friends . . . like you."

Vilho sipped his first taste and said. "It's good. I like it very much." He sipped again, then set down the glass. "I want you to teach me Russian," he said seriously. "I could gather a lot more inside information if I knew Russian. The officers know I don't understand Russian, and they talk freely like I'm not even there. I understand a word or two, but that's all. Between the two of us picking up information, we can plan resistance activity better."

Mika smiled broadly. "I'll be glad to teach you Russian. My price is one fishing trip for each five lessons."

Vilho grinned. "No problem. I'd be glad to take you fishing anytime you want to go."

Mika filled Vilho's glass. "I don't want to push you about eating but if you want duck you better order now. It's going fast."

Vilho demurred. "I know the duck would be good, but I'll wait and have something else."

A few minutes later, a group of Russian officers came in, acting a bit rowdy. Vilho noticed with some satisfaction that they were now traveling in larger groups for their own protection. Vilho watched covertly as the Russians looked around the room uneasily. He could tell by their demeanor they were more than a little nervous about the recent happenings.

Vilho said to Mika. "Those Russkies are nervous as all get out. I wonder why they don't stay home?"

Mika replied, "They're probably like little boys afraid of the dark. They're out to show us they're not afraid, but their fear is showing through."

Six more Russians came in thirty minutes later. They joined the first group, making a sizeable party. The two groups joining forces reinforced their courage along with a few too many drinks. They were very loud and rowdy. Twice Mika walked over and asked them to keep the noise level down. No results.

The third time Mika asked them to be quiet or leave, they got even more obnoxious. One of the Russians laughingly stood up and poured a beer on Mika's head. Mika took the bar cloth from his pocket to wipe his face and head. He walked behind the bar, picked up a sawed-off, double-barrelled shotgun. Cocking both hammers, he walked over to the table. The room went silent.

Mika said in his slow Russian, "Get up, you filthy pigs, and get out. If any of you that would like to die tonight, just say the word. I'll blow his brains all over this place and make the rest of you clean up the mess."

They all got up quietly and left, not making any sudden moves that might enrage this bear of a Finn further.

When they were out the door Mika blew a breath and said, "Well, there goes any further business from the Russians. I never cared much for them in the first place."

Vilho said, "I know you're going to get a visit from the commandant about this incident."

"I'm sure you're right, but this is my place, and I'll do as I damn well please. They don't have to come in here."

Mika did get a visit from no one less than Rykov himself. It was late afternoon and Mika was getting everything ready for the dinner rush. He was the only one in the dining room-bar area.

Rykov walked in arrogantly, saying, "Mika, the next time you point a shotgun at one of my men, you better reverse it and pull the trigger on yourself. I'll have you flogged on the town square. If you weren't such a well-know personage I'd have it done this time."

"You better do it right now," said Mika as he pulled the shotgun out from under the bar. In one fluid motion he levelled it at Rykov's middle with both hammers pulled back.

Rykov blanched and lost his composure completely as he looked down at the twin barrels of the deadly weapon.

Mika said, "I don't like you at all since that incident on the trail when you took my rig. Right now you're in my place and there are no witnesses. I may shoot you for the hell of it and run for the bush."

Rykov sneered, "You wouldn't dare shoot a Russian officer."

Mika poked him in the belly so hard with the shotgun that Rykov had to gasp for breath.

"You're tempting me with your damn Russian arrogance. I could shoot you and have my men take you out where no one would ever find you. They would chalk it up to the ghost murders or you leaving under too much pressure."

Rykov, visibly shaken by this time, realized that his life was in mortal danger.

Mika said, "As to this shotgun incident with your men, you better get the facts straight. First, they were disgustingly drunk and loud. I asked them three times, very politely, to keep it down. Now, I don't mind people having a good time. That's part of my business. They were bad. There were women in here, and your men were using obscene language not only in Russian but in Finnish. When one of your men poured a beer on my head, that was too much. Now you can arrest me, flog me, close me down or whatever. The minute you harm me you're going to have additional problems from my friends. I do have lots of friends. Your best choice is to forget this incident here and now. You and I are the only ones that know about this shotgun pointed at your middle. I suggest you go back and talk to your men about better behavior in the future and get them to tell you the truth. A lot of people will confirm what I said about the incident."

Rykov deciding perhaps that discretion was the better part of valor, said, "All right Mika. I'll talk to my men. Remember you're still a Russian subject and are governed by our laws."

"That's only a temporary condition. This shotgun is all I need," said Mika through gritted teeth.

Rykov was enough of a diplomat to realize he could be creating a very dangerous enemy in Mika. He didn't understand that this was already the case. He realized he was doing what he was telling his men not to do, aggravate the townspeople.

He said quietly, "I know, but for now we have to get along as best we can. I like your place and your food and so do a lot of my people. I'll see to it that they behave themselves when they come in here."

Mika calmed down when he realized that he had won the immediate battle. He also realized that he wouldn't be much use to the resistance movement if he were imprisoned and the Russians closed down his place.

He said, "All right, Major. We'll let it go at that." He eased the point of the shotgun away from the Russian officer.

Rykov let out a sigh of relief, only then realizing that he had been holding himself very tense through the entire conversation. He vowed he wouldn't let himself get into such a situation again. Without another word he turned on his heel and strode out the door.

Mika carefully let the hammers down on the shotgun and returned it to its customary place under the bar. Then he let out a long sigh of relief.

Back at the compound, Rykov called a meeting of the men who had made the complaint about Mika. As soon as they were all in his office, several of them started to sit down in chairs.

He snapped, "Stand at attention! This is not an informal meeting."

Looks of surprise came from the entire group but no one dared make any comment until they found out what it was all about.

Rykov looked slowly from man to man, not making any comments for several minutes. The men grew uneasy.

"I went out on a limb for you men and found out you hadn't given me all the facts. I talked to Mika about the shotgun incident. You men were apparently out of line in that place. I've talked to you before about aggravating the townspeople any more than absolutely necessary. You were using profanity in both Russian and Finnish with several ladies present. That wasn't good behavior for Russian officers. I also understand that one of you had the audacity to pour beer on Mika's head."

Several vehement denials and insinuations that Mika was lying came from the men. Rykov silenced the group. "Don't tell me what you did or didn't do. I talked with several witnesses who bore these facts out," lied Rykov.

Looks of apprehension passed from one to another as the men waited for the harangue that they knew would follow.

"I will have no more of these incidents," said Rykov, his voice raising with each word. "If you can't be more circumspect in your behavior, I suggest you confine your drinking to our own club. Any further incidents such as this, and you'll have to answer to me personally. Understand? Good! Dismissed!"

As soon as the men had escaped Rykov's glare and were out of earshot, the comments started in the group.

"I wonder what set him off?"

"Somebody sure put a burr under his saddle."

"I'm surprised he didn't have us go down and apologize to Mika on hands and knees."

Chekok reached Helsinki after a five-day, hard, forced ride. A few hours sleep each night was all he allowed himself. Gerchenoff wanted Golovin to know the details of the latest happening at Kiivijarvi with the Ghost Jonas episode. He hurried to headquarters to give the dispatch to Golovin personally.

Golovin acknowledged Chekok and tore open the envelope. Chekok watched as Golovin's face got redder and redder. The large vein at the side of his temple started to throb erratically before he finished the letter. Chekok was apprehensive that Golovin would have a heart attack, and he would get the blame.

Golovin threw the dispatch down on his desk, scattering other papers as leaves before the wind. He got redder in the face, calling for an orderly to get his aide, Captain Kalashnikov.

Kalashnikov came in, saluted smartly and said, "Yes sir."

"I want you to read this dispatch first. I want to talk to you about us going up there to get this mess straightened out once and for all."

Kalashnikov showed no emotion as he read through the message. He handed the dispatch back with no comment.

"How soon could you get another company of men ready to go. I plan on going up there to supervise the entire operation. This incident is getting too far out of hand. The tsar is shouting about getting one Finn that's spreading dissent throughout the land."

"Within the week," the captain said, "if we go with one of the companies already on alert."

"See what you can get done and report back to me. You both can go. Kalashnikov, would you show Chekok to some suitable quarters?"

He snapped, "Yes sir," as he saluted and took Chekok by the arm and out the door.

"Do you really think Golovin is going to go to Kiivijarvi?" asked Chekok.

"Not if I can help it," said Kalashnikov. "I don't want to go up there, and I don't think he can do any better than Rykov and Gerchenoff. I have to make Golovin think it's his idea to stay here. He's a good administrator, but he's no field soldier, and I don't want to leave Helsinki myself."

"Do you have any idea how you're going to make him think it's his idea to stay here?"

"Not yet. What about you? Got any good ideas?"

"None right now, but Rykov and Gerchenoff don't want him up there. They say they have more supervision than they need."

"I'm going to try to convince him to send that company back with you in command, but I don't know how I am going to get it done."

They arrived at the officers' quarters and Kalashnikov showed Chekok to an empty room.

"If you'd like, we could go out some place for dinner and talk about our mutual problem."

"That would suit me fine. First I'm going to a sauna I used to use. I need to wash five days sweat and horse smell off my body."

Chekok shook his clothes out, selected a clean uniform and under clothes and headed for the sauna. He thought about a woman, but he was more interested in getting clean.

Back at his room he waited for Kalashnikov. He was getting hungry as he had skipped lunch to deliver the dispatch to Golovin.

Kalashnikov showed up. He also had changed his uniform. He looked every inch the professional soldier, tall, dark haired with a small moustache, well muscled with a flat stomach. It looked to Chekok like Golovin wanted the contrast. Rykov was much the same in looks and military bearing.

"Are you ready to go? I thought we would go to the Boar's Head. I know you've been there. The ex-owner has a new place in Kiivijarvi . . . by the same name, I believe. The place here is pretty much the same, not quite as good as it was with Mika running it."

"Anything sounds good to me right now, I'm really hungry."

They walked to the Boar's Head talking about how they could convince Golovin not to go to Kiivijarvi.

The next day Kalashnikov mentioned casually to Golovin, "I had an excellent meal with Chekok. I'm going to miss all this when we go to Kiivijarvi."

Golovin took the bait a little bit as he said wistfully, "You're right, Helsinki is not St. Petersburg, but then Kiivijarvi is not Helsinki either. I wish they would get with it up there and catch Jonas. We're getting reports from other areas about people ignoring our directives. We think it's because they see Jonas making fools of us at every turn."

Kalashnikov said, "I think Rykov and Gerchenoff are doing about everything they can. That Jonas is a smart old fox. I know how bad Rykov wants to come back. If there was any way he could end it, I'm sure he would."

Kalashnikov had planted the seed and was going to sit back and let it grow.

The next morning Golovin called Chekok and Kalashnikov in for a meeting.

"Chekok, you've been up there and know the operation. Do you think I could help it more up there or staying down here?"

"Well sir, I'm not that much on tactics, but it looks like Rykov and Gerchenoff are doing everything there is to do. The extra troops might help, give them more manpower to cover more ground."

"That's somewhat my position. I was thinking about going up there myself, but I can help more from here with men and supplies," said Golovin.

Kalashnikov breathed a sigh of relief and said, "I have the troops ready to go, but we'll need a few more days to get the extra supplies. I would suggest we put Chekok in charge of that unit as he's familiar with the route and the situation in Kiivijarvi."

"Excellent suggestion," said Golovin. "Make that up into an order and I'll sign it. Congratulations on your new command Chekok. There'll be a promotion to go with it."

"Thank you sir. I appreciate the vote of confidence."

"I would suggest the two of you explore the logistics of getting the unit ready to go. Dismissed."

They both saluted, and Golovin returned a perfunctory salute as he returned to the paper work on his desk.

The preparations for the move went without a hitch due to Kalashnikov's knowledge of everything in the area. He wanted the troops to get on the way before Golovin could change his mind about going to Kiivijarvi.

Leslie W. Wisuri

The day before departure Golovin received a dispatch from no less a personage than the tsar. It was essentially Golovin's death sentence as to future promotions unless he managed to solve the problem of Jonas quickly. He knew he should go on to Kiivijarvi, but he couldn't tear himself away from Helsinki and its comforts. He was going to send the extra troops and hope it would suffice.

That afternoon Golovin had Chekok, Kalashnikov, and the other officers and non-commissioned officers scheduled to depart for Kiivijarvi come in for a briefing. Kalashnikov was not going with the troops, but Golovin wanted him to hear the message.

"Men," he began, "In my hand I have a paper written by our illustrious leader, Tsar Nicholas the II. Normally, I would be more than pleased to hear from him, but this directive is of a little different nature. Let me read it.

> To: The Finnish High Command.
> Attention Colonel Golovin.
> From: Nicholas the II Tsar of all the Russias.
> Subject: Jonas Kekola, one rebel Finnish soldier.
>
> It was brought to my attention very forcibly several times in recent months of your and our inability to apprehend this Finnish subject. The one who had the audacity to murder one of our officers. Then, you let him escape to do further damage and murder more Russians by various means. This latest series of murders has me concerned that this kind of behavior will spread all over the land.
>
> All the reports I have read to date smacks of incompetence among the Finnish area commanders. Colonel Golovin, as first in command, I am holding you personally responsible for this problem. The rest of you, officers and enlisted men, down the line must shoulder responsibility to some degree. Every one of you has been incompetent in some way or else this renegade would be dead and this whole incident forgotten.
>
> I am, this date, charging all of you with renewed effort and courage to go forth to apprehend this man. Bring glory once more to the name of Russia in the Finnish province.

41

I will brook no excuses why this can not be done. In the next few months I expect this incident to be forgotten in Russian history.

Signed Nicholas the II Tsar of all the Russias.

Golovin lowered the missive and made eye contact with those in the room. "I will send this proclamation on to Major Rykov to read to the rest of the troops in Kiivijarvi," he said. "I ask that you bend all efforts toward the tsar's task before us. I not only ask it, I demand it! We have put this group together as the best Mother Russia has to offer. I will not tolerate a disappointment in this matter. Dismissed."

*   *   *   *   *

The party left the next morning, bound for Kiivijarvi. When they arrived, Rykov and Gerchenoff were pleased Golovin had not come. They heaped praise on Chekok, who took it as though he had done it all, but it was Kalashnikov who really had gotten the job done. The extra troops were a welcomed assistance in the search for Jonas as they could put more men in the field at a time.

Chapter Four

First Raid

VILHO WAS SPENDING A LOT OF TIME with Mika learning Russian. He was a very apt student, and he made progress quickly. Early one afternoon, he entered the Boar's Head Tavern. Mika, the only one there at the moment, looked up. Vilho greeted him in Russian, and Mika responded in kind.

"How goes the struggle?"

"It goes as it goes," Vilho answered back in very good Russian.

They both laughed and slapped each other on the back with Mika saying, "You make a better Russian than most Russians."

"Well, I have a good teacher."

"I hope you don't get so Russian oriented that you start smelling like one."

"Never fear, Mika, I like my saunas too much, and I do hate their stench."

"We're getting a few of them used to using saunas. You can tell which ones use them," said Mika.

"The last time Jonas was home, he said he hoped the Russians didn't use our saunas as he wouldn't be able to smell them coming. He told me he could smell them a long way if the wind was just right. Between their body odor and the tar on their boots, they do have a quite distinctive smell."

"Are you picking up anything around the Russian officers about Jonas or events in general?" asked Mika.

"Quite a lot, in fact. I'm amazed how much you taught me. I miss a word or phrase now and then, but most of the time I get enough of it. The tsar wrote a paper to all the troops in Finland. I don't know exactly what's in it, but everyone's up in the air about going all out to get Jonas. Major Rykov has taken over the entire operation. I haven't had much contact with him yet, but I understand he's a soldier's soldier."

"You need to know what he's like under adverse conditions. His fancy-trail rig burned on the way up here, and he confiscated mine. If he had asked, I would have loaned it to him. He ordered Elsa and me out of the rig without any apologies. I don't care for him at all."

"I heard he's a tough taskmaster and doesn't give a damn if the troops like him as long as they do their job."

"The Major Rykov, I know, is a real stinker about handling men. He doesn't care one iota about their feelings. He's one of the few men I dislike in this world. He's a real force to contend with in relation to our operations here. We ought to kill him right now before he causes too much trouble."

Mika got a couple of cold beers in mugs while they continued their lessons. They spent the next couple of hours conversing back and forth in Russian. Mika made a few trips to the kitchen to check on dinner preparations.

Mika said, "I don't know how much more Russian I can teach you. You're doing very well. Listen to them talk. If you don't understand, try to remember the word or phrase and how they used it, and I'll try to translate later. The best way to learn is by talking like we've been doing right now."

"I really appreciate all the help. It'll help in keeping tabs on what's going on with the Russians. For right now, how about fixing me something to eat. Just throw something together."

Mika returned a few minutes later with a plate of sliced cold beef, steaming hot, fresh bread with a big glass of buttermilk.

Vilho said, "Looks good, Mika. You even remembered how much I like buttermilk."

Mika winked. "That's a sign of a good business man. Never forget what your customers like."

Vilho ate and lingered for a while watching the customers dribbling into the tavern. A few more Russian officers than usual sat among the patrons. They behaved well enough. Vilho concluded that Mika's use of the double barrel and Rykov's tirade had improved their behavior.

A group of six officers entered, ordered wine first and sat down at a table close to Vilho. Vilho was about to leave but changed his mind. This would be a good chance to eavesdrop and improve his own Russian. He got up to get himself a beer refill, waving to Mika that he was not going to leave. Mika waved back to show he understood.

Vilho eavesdropped the idle chitchat and was about to give up gleaning anything of value.

Then one of the officers asked, "What do you think of the new American-made repeating rifles we're getting?"

Another one said, "I'll know better after next week when we get them and I have a chance to fire one."

A third one said, "It doesn't look like this first shipment will be big enough to get everyone outfitted. Eventually, we'll all have them."

The conversation drifted on to other topics about Mika's place and lack of entertainment. They talked about the Finnish women and their poor interest in Russian men.

Vilho smiled to himself thinking what they would say if they knew he was listening to their every word.

One of the men said, "The entertainment may not be great up here but we do get to see and use all the latest equipment available. The food is the best that can be had anywhere. They do take care of the troops on a special problem like this one. Just think, all this effort to catch one man."

Vilho smiled slightly, thinking, *If they only knew that the one man they hunted was nowhere within their grasp, they would be terribly disappointed. If they knew how the concept of one Ghost was going to become hundreds and hundreds of freedom fighters all over Finland, they might not think their duty so good.*

Vilho's mind had fixed on the mention of the new rifles coming into the area. He was curious why the American rifle was being imported. He thought perhaps the encounters with Jonas had convinced the Russians they needed something else. Usually the Russians bought French rifles and powder. He didn't know how they could know Jonas had an American rifle unless he had left an empty cartridge case somewhere, and this was unlikely. At any rate Vilho made up his mind to find out more about the shipment of rifles. He stayed until closing time, hoping to hear more, but all he got was idle conversation. He did miss a couple of words that he wanted to ask Mika about, and he wanted to discuss the new rifles with him.

Mika finally asked the Russians to leave as it was closing time. Vilho made no move to go, and the Russians asked pointedly why he wasn't leaving.

Mika put a hand on Vilho's shoulder saying, "This is a friend of mine, and he can stay as long as he wants."

The Russians grumbled but left.

When they were alone in the tavern, Mika said, "It's absolutely amazing what a double-barrel shotgun will do for teaching those Russians some manners. I'm quite certain that they got the word from the other group plus a lecture from Gerchenoff or Rykov."

Vilho told Mika about hearing the conversation of the rifles.

"This might be a chance to give the resistance group some experience and get some modern arms."

"I thought the same," said Vilho, "But I don't know anything except that they're coming in next week. If they're heavily guarded, we would be foolish to try anything."

46

"Let's not give up too soon. See if you can find out anything more about the shipment. We'll see if there's anything we can do about a possible unauthorized requisition."

They talked into the early morning about their newly formed and untried group of resisters and how that group might relieve the Russians of their gun shipment.

Vilho, yawning, said, "I hate to break this up, Mika, but if I'm to learn about the shipment, I better get some sleep."

"I didn't realize it was so late. These long summer days keep me confused. I'll see you tomorrow night," said Mika.

Vilho stood. "I wish I could read Russian. I might be able to pick up something off Gerchenoff's desk."

"The reading comes next. For now just listen. Besides it would be a little dangerous if they caught you rifling through papers even though they don't think you understand the language."

The next day Vilho hung around the officers as much as possible trying to get some clue about the gun shipment. During breaks he lolled around underneath the orderly room window but to no avail.

The news he needed ended up coming from a completely unexpected source. Arne, one of his friends, approached him to ask if he knew anything about some new guns coming in for the Russians.

Vilho very excitedly asked, "Where did you hear about that?"

"It's all over. Some new American guns are coming in tomorrow night. A couple of us have to stay late to help them unload."

"What time do they expect them to come in?"

"I don't know, but Gerchenoff said that we should be through before eight as there were only two wagons. Why?"

"I could use the extra duty. But if they already told you then I guess I'm not on the roster."

"I didn't hear your name mentioned."

Later that day Vilho had the information verified when he overheard Gerchenoff and Rykov discussing the shipment.

They ignored him as though he wasn't there. Little did they know he understood everything they said. Now he had confirmation from two sources.

Vilho was anxious to get off duty and tell Mika about the shipment. When Gerchenoff dismissed the troops, he hurried to the Boar's Head to share what he had learned. "The shipment is coming in by the old river road tomorrow night but I don't know what time or how many guards or anything else. Arne is on a special detail to help unload the wagons, and there are only two of them. They'll be done unloading by eight o'clock. That should give us some idea of their arrival time."

Mika laughed and said, "I hope we can save Arne all that back breaking labor by unloading them ourselves."

Vilho said, "I think I have a plan, but it involves work, back-breaking work. We'll need manpower to pull it off."

"What do you have in mind?" asked Mika.

"Well, we'll need a trough of heavy boards about twenty feet long strong enough to support a case of rifles. We'll need two wagons just like their regular freight wagons and a light buggy of some kind so long as it has a different track than our wagons or theirs. We'll need ten good men we can trust, some rope to tie up the Russians, and some masks for our crew."

"I still don't see what you have in mind," said Mika.

"You will. You will. I don't have time to explain it all right now. We'll have the Russians scratching their heads over this one for a long time. Get the men and be thinking of a place where we can leave the guns without them getting wet. The other criterion needed is hard ground. We can't leave deep tracks. The wagons are going to be heavy. I hope there's ammunition with the shipment."

Mika said, "I can think of two places that might be good for storing the guns. There's the old Niemi farm east of town. I was going to buy it before the house burned. The barn is still there. There's also that old cabin on the rock quarry road."

"The rock quarry road sounds best. They have heavy wagons on that road all the time. It wouldn't matter about our wagon

48

tracks other than those going into the cabin itself. Is there anyone in our group who works at the quarry?"

"One or two, I think."

"That would be great. They could keep an eye on the cabin until we can distribute the guns to our people."

"I can't get away from here tonight to contact any of our people so it's going to have to be up to you. Let's pick the ten most reliable and include whoever works at the quarry," said Mika.

They drew up a list of the men they needed.

Mika said, pointing to the list, "These two will be in here tonight, so I can talk to them, but the rest are up to you."

"All right. I know where they all live. Several of them have riding horses which we'll need, but I can make those arrangements. I'm on my way. See you after a while," said Vilho going out the door.

Vilho made contact with the men on his list. All agreed, as he knew they would, to take part in the raid. Vilho then returned to the Boar's Head. Mika had contacted the other two men, so the crew was complete.

Vilho said, "I got the two heavy wagons and most of the rest we'll need. What about the trough? If I can get you the approximate dimensions, can you get it made in time?"

Mika assured him he could.

Vilho went home to get ready for the raid. He hoped he could get into the supply depot to look at the gun crate of American guns sent in advance of the full shipment. He half remembered seeing one marked USA and Winchester near the main door. This was the one he needed for the dimensions. He wished he had paid more attention to it the first time he saw it.

The next morning he went to the supply depot ostensibly looking for his friend Arne. The men there hadn't seen Arne, but the gun case in question was right where he remembered. He couldn't measure it but his carpenter's practiced eye gave him a good idea. The trough could be larger but not smaller than the gun crates, so he would make sure it was large enough.

The next problem was getting the dimensions to Mika during lunch break. He looked up Urho, one of the resisters he had contacted, who usually rode his horse to the compound. He found the man and asked to borrow the horse.

"No problem. She's tethered right behind the main stables. The saddle and bridle are by the corner of the stables. Is it information about tonight?"

"Yes, it is."

"God speed then. I'll see you tonight."

Vilho had to forego lunch to get the information to Mika and still get back in time for duty. He told Mika, "We told everyone to be prompt, but if you see any of the crew remind them how important it is. I'll do the same. Looks like we'll have a couple of hours to get everything ready."

Mika said, "We can be ready by then. Let's hope they didn't make better time with the wagons than we planned."

"It won't matter if they're late as we'll have all night once we get into position, but early could be a problem. Here are the measurements for the trough and a little drawing to help."

Mika looked at the drawing and dimensions and said, "Simple enough, I'll have it for you this afternoon. I took the liberty of making masks for you and your men. They're going to look like ghosts to carry on with the ghost symbol we've been using."

"I didn't know you were a seamstress too. Your talents never cease to amaze me."

"When you're a bachelor, you have to learn all kinds of strange chores," said Mika laughing.

With that Vilho leaped on his horse and galloped back to camp.

With a little time to spare, he talked to the men about the evening raid.

"You two wagon drivers, I want you to fill your wagons with rocks. Don't fill them so full it's obvious, though. Fill them level to the side boards."

"What are we going to do with the rocks?"

"You'll see tonight."

Jacob, one of the wagon drivers said. "The rocks are no problem. I have all you want on my farm."

Vilho said, "Don't get really big ones. Get ones we can handle easily. See you tonight."

That afternoon Vilho had the opportunity to eavesdrop on some officers again.

The first officer said, "I heard the new guns are coming in tonight. We should get to try them in a day or two."

The second one said, "A lot of good that first case was without ammunition. We couldn't even try them out. I understand we're getting quite a bit of ammunition with this shipment. There are reloading tools so we can reload the empties. This will eliminate a long wait for another shipment of ammunition from America."

They chatted back and forth about the merits of the new rifles over the old, obsolete single-shot ones they were using.

Vilho took it all in. The additional information delighted him, especially finding out they would have reloading equipment with them. That was a real bonus. It would make it easier for the resistance group to keep using the guns if they did manage to get them.

The afternoon dragged by as if tethered to a post. Vilho itched to get the shift over with so he could get an early start on the project. At quitting time, Gerchenoff took the time to give the men a pep talk on the virtues of being good soldiers for Mother Russia. He droned on and on, with everyone getting fidgety. Vilho eyed the men going with him on the raid and saw that they were getting nervous. Vilho was sure the paper from the tsar had a lot to do with the talk they were now receiving.

He thought. "If Gerchenoff doesn't wind this up soon, I think I'll go out of my mind. If he only knew what we're planning, he would really try to delay us. I wonder what the talk will be about tomorrow if we pull this off tonight?"

After a long time, lots of pauses, and cliches, Gerchenoff told the first sergeant to dismiss the men.

Vilho wanted to run to Mika to see if he got the trough done and had contacted the other men that were to go on the raid. He hurried as fast as he could without being obvious.

As he entered the Boar's head, Mika said, "It's all done and ready to go out back."

They both walked to the back, talking about the raid.

Vilho inspected the trough. "It looks good. Just what I had in mind."

Mika said, "I made arrangements to be off tonight so I could go with you. I really want to do my share."

Vilho said vehemently, "No, Mika. As much as I would like your expertise, we can't take a chance on you getting caught. We need you more right here. When this is over, the Russians will want to know where everyone was at the time. You would be so conspicuous by your absence that they would be looking for you first."

Mika pondered silently for a few minutes and said sorrowfully, "I suppose you're right, Vilho, but I did want to go in the worst way."

"Well, that's what it would be, the worst way. You're valuable to the movement right where you are. If it weren't for you teaching me Russian, I wouldn't have been able to eavesdrop that first conversation and learn about the shipment. You just stay here and hold down the fort."

Just then one of the wagons came around the back to pick up the chute. They loaded it in the wagon, said goodbye to Mika and were on their way.

Mika waved and shouted, "Good luck. See you later."

When they got to the clearing by the river road, the rest of the men were waiting.

The clearing was small and off the main road. Apparently, it had been the start of someone's dream as there were the remains of a small cabin falling in on itself. Some of the land had been cleared but the cabin was never completed. The trees surrounding the place had grown thick, making the spot invisible from the main road.

Vilho stood up in his wagon to address the men.

"I'm glad you're here. I know we all think the same so I won't dwell on that right now. We don't have much time. I'll go through the plan quickly so everyone will know their job.

"First, the two heavy wagons will stay here until we need them. The light buggy with John driving it, will go down to the river and park. If anyone shows up, act as though you were just getting through an unsuccessful fishing trip. John, let the wagons come on through and then head to Mika's. If anyone asks, you didn't see anything suspicious. If there's a heavy detachment with the wagons, one you think we can't handle, jump in your buggy and pass the wagons, heading this way. We'll see you go through first and let the wagons pass. If it looks good, go to Mika's and stay there. If you don't have questions, John, you better get going now so you'll be in place before the shipment comes through."

John nodded and left. Vilho continued to explain the plan to the remaining men. "The rest of us will go down the road to the bend just above the river but out of sight of the river bridge. When the shipment arrives, we'll step out with our masks on and guns in hand to make them stop. Once we have the Russians secure, we'll take them into the woods, tie and gag them. Urho will stay with them to make sure no one gets loose before we get through.

"Heiki, you watch for us coming up the road with the Russian wagons. When you see us, run back and signal our wagons to start moving this way. As soon as the first wagon passes, move the wagon with the chute directly behind the first wagon and as close as you can get. We run the trough between the horses to the back of the Russian wagon. We should be able to push the rifle boxes down the chute easily enough. At the same time start transferring rocks into the Russian wagon. It's going to be heavy work, but we have to move quickly.

"As soon as the first wagon is done, we'll transfer the chute to our second wagon which should be in position in front of the second Russian wagon. Again we transfer rocks and guns. We want the Russian wagon loaded with rocks to keep the wheel marks the same. We want it clear that the wagons never left the road. After the transfer, the marks of the extra wagons should be erased from the road. Then all four wagons will proceed to the rock quarry crossroad, trying to keep to the same ruts. When we get there, our wagons will turn off. Aero will jump down and brush out all marks of our wagons turning off. John will be by with his buggy to turn at the same place so the rub outs will not be obvious.

"The rest of you will stay with the wagons. As soon as we pass the crossroad, start lightening the Russian wagons by throwing rocks out into the ditches.

"You two on horseback will ride up to the wagons, stay with them for a few feet then ride off into the woods and back again. We want it to look as though you were lifting crates off and dropping them in the woods.

"When you've emptied all the rocks, come back to the quarry cabin to help us unload. We want the Russians to think we unloaded the guns and ammunition by horseback and dropped them in the woods. The longer we can keep them thinking that the better.

"You two on horseback will ride to the next heavily traveled crossroad. From there, I want you to go home with your horses. Turn them loose and get to the Boar's head as quickly as possible so you'll have an alibi. They'll think we couldn't unload all those rifles and ammunition as quickly as we will and make it to the Boar's Head.

"The problem is the heavy wagons. I think we'll be all right if you drivers take the backroads home. Then meet at the Boar's Head. As soon as all the rocks are out of the Russian wagons, sweep them down, tie the reins to the wagon seat and turn the horses loose. They'll find their way back to the stables.

"Mika made masks for all of us but the only ones who need them are those in contact with the Russians. The white masks will perpetuate the ghost legend of Jonas. He's our inspiration and symbol for freedom.

"All right. Let's get on with it."

They moved out to await the coming of the wagons. They didn't have long to wait. They heard the yelling and cursing of the Russian teamsters and then they heard the wagons as they rumbled across the bridge.

Vilho looked around at his men and saw a little nervousness. He expected this on their first mission. He nodded to the men to don their masks. Each man pulled on his mask adjusting the eye holes so they could see. The wagons came closer, unaware of the men waiting in ambush. Vilho was relieved to see there were only three men per wagon.

As the wagons pulled abreast of his position Vilho stepped from behind a tree, rifle at the ready. He gave the command to halt and dismount in Russian. When they hesitated slightly, Vilho gave the signal for the rest of the men to step out.

He said in his best Russian, "I'm sure you don't want to die this day for a handful of rifles."

The Russians stepped down gingerly not wanting to make any sudden, threatening moves. They were quickly herded into the woods where they were bound and gagged. Vilho signaled to Urho to take over while the rest went up the road with the wagons.

From that point on everything went like clockwork. They spread the Russian wagons out enough to accommodate their own wagon between them. The first wagon pulled into place, and the cargos were exchanged in record time. It took a little time to transfer the chute from the first pair of wagons to the second without getting to the ground. It was done while the wagons were moving. Vilho wished he had used two chutes instead of one but this was working out quite well. All cargo was transferred before they reached their turn off. At no time did they encounter anyone on the road. This had been Vilho's greatest worry.

Vilho's wagons reached the quarry cabin without incident. The old floor boards were removed to dig a space to accommodate the guns and ammunition. Then the wagons were hauled away and the dirt smoothed so as not to leave any outward signs of recent disturbance.

The men driving the Russian wagons and throwing away the rocks showed up to report that all was well and that the horses were slowly plodding their way to the stables.

The boards over the cabin hole were put back in place with dust and weeds scattered over the area to make it look undisturbed. Everyone prepared to leave in a different direction to rendevous at the Boar's Head.

Before they left Vilho warned everyone, "Let's not all sit together at the Boar's Head. Act natural, say hello to the others as they come in as if you hadn't seen them for a while. Stay until the Russians come to check on everyone's whereabouts then leave at different intervals. I'll stay until after closing, which I usually do anyway.

"We want it to look like we have been at the tavern for most of the evening. They'll know what time their shipment was due, but they'll have no way to know we could move all those guns so quickly and be at the Boar's Head. All right. Let's move out."

Pandemonium broke loose when the empty wagons showed up at the stables. There wasn't a single doubt these were the wagons carrying the new rifles.

Gerchenoff was informed, who in turn sent a runner to tell Rykov. The two officers met at the stables to look over the wagons. Gerchenoff, the first to arrive, was only half dressed. Rykov arrived a few minutes later, fully clothed in an immaculate uniform as always.

Rykov asked, "What in hell's going on? Where are the rifles? Where are the men?"

Typically Rykov asked about the rifles before he thought about the welfare of the men.

Gerchenoff answered, "I don't know. The sentry just reported the empty wagons to me."

"We still have a little daylight left. Get a patrol mounted immediately. We still might have time to catch the theives. What was their route?" snapped Rykov.

Gerchenoff sent a runner to alert the first and second platoons. He was a firm believer in getting more men than needed for a job.

The men from the two platoons reported for duty. When they heard of the problem they ran for their horses. Neither Rykov nor Gerchenoff was aware that they were playing right into the raiders' hands. Having that many men and horses milling about would obscure all signs.

Rykov said, "Get a tracker. On second thought, get two. If this is Jonas, it might be trickier than we think."

Mounts were brought for Rykov and Gerchenoff. Gerchenoff sent an orderly for his clothes. He put on his shirt and uniform jacket as they rode down the river road.

Half way to the river bridge, they met the teamsters and escort just as they managed to get themselves loose.

"We were held up by fifteen or twenty masked men," said one of the drivers.

Rykov barked orders right and left. "Two of you come with me. Show me where this happened. Mount those teamsters double on the horses and have them look at the wagons to see if there's anything different. Get foot patrols down here to help us search the area. Move out!"

They arrived at the actual hold up area a few minutes later. Rykov had everyone stand back while the trackers did their work.

Shortly, one of the trackers came back and said, "They stood around in this area for some time and then boarded the wagons right here. I don't believe there were over ten men at the most. A light buggy came after the wagons but that's all that's passed here lately."

One of the escort men spoke up. "That buggy was down by the river when we came through. He was loading his fishing gear. There's no way they could have loaded all those guns into that light buggy."

"Find him," snapped Rykov. "He may have seen something. Track down who was fishing."

The trackers moved toward town, one on each side of the road. They passed the quarry road with out seeing anything suspicious.

One tracker came back and said, "Sir, I believe they started unloading about here to men on horseback. It looks like the wagons are getting lighter. The horse tracks come to the wagons and then leave, going off into the woods."

Rykov said, "I bet they broke open the cases and moved the guns that way. Get that foot patrol into the woods. See if they can find where they hid the guns. They couldn't have moved that much stuff by horseback that quick for any distance."

Men and horses trampled the area obliterating all tracks. It would be impossible to find out just what did happen.

Rykov and Gerchenoff rode up and down the road checking trackers, mounted patrols, and foot soldiers for possible clues to no avail.

Rykov was getting angrier by the minute. "Damn it, those guns have to be close by somewhere. It would have taken half the town to move them away from here that quickly. There's not one shred of evidence of them using wagons of any kind."

The other tracker reported to Rykov, "They have definitely been unloading the wagons as they went. The tracks keep getting shallower all the time, meaning they're losing weight."

The search continued until near midnight when the short summer night came upon them. They reconvened at daylight. They concentrated all efforts on the area past the quarry road where there was nothing to be found.

Belatedly one of the teamsters remarked that at least one of the thieves, clearly the leader, spoke fluent Russian.

Rykov exploded. "Why in hell didn't you mention this before?"

"I didn't think it was that important."

Rykov called Gerchenoff over to explain the latest bit of news, "This man says the leader spoke fluent Russian. Hell, one of our men could have turned traitor, or they could all be Russians looking to make a quick profit by selling those guns. Very few, if any of the Finns speak Russian. The only one I know is Mika, and anyone would have recognized his pot belly. Our man says the leader was tall and thin. I don't know how the Finns could know about the shipment. It would have been easy for our men to find out all the details. Most have known about those guns for weeks. Hell, we've had training sessions on the ones we got earlier."

Gerchenoff said, "Looks like we're going to have a double-barreled investigation going on here."

"What about those ghost masks they used?" asked Rykov.

"If it was our men, what better way to throw off suspicion than to have it look like the Jonas group. Everyone knew about the ghost symbols found on the men killed for killing Crazy Jake."

The next day, all the resisters involved in the raid laughed quietly to themselves as they watched the antics of the Russians trying to figure out what happened.

That evening, Vilho and Mika toasted the success of the mission. Vilho said, "It went even better than I planned. Not only are the Russians thoroughly confused as to what happened, they think it might be some of their own men because I spoke in Russian. This is the second time your teaching me Russian has really paid off."

"I wish I could have been there," said Mika wistfully.

Chapter Five

Escape

THE RUSSIANS SUSPECTED VILHO to be the killer of Aimo, a Finnish enlisted man who was an informer for the Russians. The killing of the Russians after Crazy Jake's death did not go unnoticed either.

The guard Vilho had slugged and dragged behind the lumber pile had gained consciousness before Vilho left the barracks. He saw Vilho on his way out. For several weeks, the guard said nothing as he feared for his life. After continued questioning, however, he finally admitted seeing Vilho leave. This didn't prove that Vilho was the killer, only that he was in the area.

Vilho didn't know the guard had seen him. When weeks without anyone questioning him, he thought he was safe.

Rykov, however, quietly gathered several trusted officers and enlisted men to take Vilho into custody. He wanted to avoid repercussions from the Finnish people.

The simplest plan, as always, was the best. Rykov had Vilho and several other men report for special duty. They planned to grab him as soon as he entered the compound and then dismiss the other men. They planned to question him, then imprison him to await a firing squad in the morning. To them, there was no doubt about the guilt of Vilho. The questioning was only a formality.

The men filed into the orderly room. When they were all inside, they asked Vilho to step into Rykov's office. The first sergeant quietly dismissed the rest of the men.

Vilho knew immediately that something was wrong when he saw four other men in the room with Rykov. Two stood guard by the door.

Rykov said quietly, "Sit down Vilho. We have a few questions to ask you regarding the death of some Russian officers."

Vilho blanched inwardly but showed no emotion to the officers and men who were watching his reactions very closely.

Rykov continued, "We know you killed the officers in the barracks. You were seen leaving the area by the guard you hit on the head. We are reasonably sure you're the one who killed Malenkov on the road."

Vilho said quietly. "You're mistaken. I have never been near the officers' barracks at night."

Rykov pushed his face right into Vilho's, shouting, "Don't try to lie! I didn't say it was done at night. You might as well confess now because there's nothing you can say at this point to save yourself. We're going to shoot you in the morning!"

Vilho flinched inwardly as he didn't think they would do anything to him so soon. He replied very calmly, "I wouldn't give you that satisfaction even if I had done it. You've made up your mind I did it."

The calmness of Vilho infuriated Rykov. Before Vilho could put up any defense, Rykov back handed him across the mouth. A small trickle of blood appeared at the corner of his mouth. Vilho calmly wiped the blood away with a slight smile on his lips. This infuriated Rykov even more. He hit him with a doubled up fist, knocking him off his chair.

He shouted, "Pick yourself up, you Finnish pig!"

This time the steely glint of anger appeared in Vilho's eyes as he picked himself up and sat down.

Rykov strode around to his desk, trying to regain his composure. He stood there for several minutes clenching and unclenching his fists, looking at Vilho with absolute hatred. After a lengthy silence, he began to calm down. Rykov's anger rose because he couldn't intimidate Vilho even with the threat of death.

Vilho knew he should do something, as his death was very near if he did nothing. Many thoughts of escape raced through his mind. He knew if he wound up in prison, they would guard him closely until his execution because of the escape Jonas had made earlier.

Rykov came from behind the desk, pacing back and forth in front of Vilho, shooting questions at him rapidly, really not expecting or even waiting for any answers. The process seemed more to vent his pent up anger and emotions than extract information.

Rykov changed his tactics from ranting and raving to cajoling saying, "If you saw fit to lead us to Jonas, we would spare your miserable life."

Vilho looked blankly at Rykov as if he were completely out of his mind, knowing full well Jonas was safe in America. He thought momentarily about leading them on a wild goose chase for Jonas.

Rykov's anger grew again, and he leaned over Vilho with both hands resting on the arms of Vilho's chair while he shouted directly into his face. "You bastard of a Finn, you will regret this and lose your life."

Vilho saw his chance, slim though it was. He kicked hard into Rykov's groin. His foot caught the officer just right, and Rykov howled with pain, falling to the floor. Vilho wasted no time. He jumped up, taking three long steps across the room and dove for the window. Glass and window framing went with him. He hit the ground outside in a roll and did a complete somersault. He came to his feet like a cat, running for freedom. The men in the orderly room shouted out the window for someone to stop him, but there were only Finns outside; the men made no move to stop Vilho in his headlong flight out of the compound.

The Russians poured from the orderly room, getting into each other's way, which further slowed a rapid pursuit.

Vilho ran as fast as he could for the board fence surrounding the compound, hoping that the "back door" or hole under the fence was still there. Enlisted men used the hole to go into town without a pass.

By this time the pursuit was getting organized and streaking across the compound in full chase. Several of the Russians were fleet of foot and gaining on Vilho.

Vilho hit the fence, finding the hole under it still open. After he crawled through, he took time to tumble a large boulder into the hole to slow pursuit. The rock sat where it was difficult to move from the other side. The Russians gave up trying to move it and sped toward the nearest gate, giving Vilho a considerable head start.

Vilho hit the woods still running, allowing himself a sigh of relief but no rest. The entire group would try to track him down, and they weren't far behind. For the moment, though, all that concerned him were the runners. Soon they would be coming out the gate. He assumed the runners would come to the hole in the fence and would deduce he ran away from the gate. He ran toward the gate flopping down in the nearest thicket to catch his breath. The runners ran right past him. As soon as they were out of sight, he ran in the other direction, plunging deeper into the woods. He knew he would wind up at Jonas' and Emma's old cabin, but he didn't want to lead his pursuers to the area.

The woods would be swarming with searchers for a few days. He didn't want to go to the cabin until the heat was off. As he ran, he thought about living off the land the way his friend Jonas had. He had no gun, no American rifle, like Jonas. The only weapon he had was the knife on his belt. It was summertime so at least it wouldn't be too much of a problem keeping warm and finding plenty to eat.

The Russians quickly organized a full-scale search. Rykov, still recuperating from the kick in the groin, barked orders right and left while doubled over in pain and suffering lots of humiliation.

Vilho headed for the lakes area north and west of town. This was an area far from the Jonas cabin, plus it was an area he knew very well. He knew he could evade his pursuers, catch fish and find berries to survive for a time. He was sure the Russians would start their search south and east. This was the most logical search area based on where he came through the compound fence.

Rykov still grimacing in pain took over the search. He directed the search to start with the dogs south and east of the hole hoping to save time. They lost a considerable amount of time before they went back to the hole. Then they found where he had doubled back into the face of his pursuers.

Rykov was fuming about the lost time, "He's just like his cohort, Jonas. The old fox is doing just the opposite of what we would expect."

Vilho knew they would use dogs, and it wouldn't be long before they unravelled his trail. He was far enough in front of his pursuers so he did not have to worry about immediate capture. He had to think of how he was going to fool the dogs.

Rykov said to no one in particular, "One item in our favor is that he has no weapon other than his knife."

Vilho considered getting a rifle and ammunition from the ones they raided, but if they tracked him to the site, they would lose the whole lot. He made up his mind to rely on his wits and woodsmanship to elude his pursuers. He settled into an easy trot, following the high ridges toward the lake country. He formulated a plan as he ran.

Rykov reduced his search group down to twenty men and four dogs. He thought about turning out the whole camp, but a group that large would be unwieldy and would alert Vilho of their coming much sooner. Tracks and scents would be lost before they found the right way to search.

Vilho got his second wind and was breathing easier, covering a tremendous amount of ground, putting more distance between himself and his pursuers. He knew he was leaving a good odor path for the dogs because of his exertion but he felt distance was more important. The smaller odor path would not slow them that much anyway.

The Rykov group was making fairly good time. The dog handlers were moving at a brisk walk with the rest of the group following behind.

Rykov was irritated as he was still hurting from the kick in the groin. He was badly out of condition from his long stints of desk sitting. He was having a hard time keeping up with the group but didn't want to show weakness to his troops. Rykov called a halt to give himself some rest and voice the question uppermost in everyone's mind, "Why isn't he trying to hide his trail better? Is he leading us into some kind of trap?"

"What possible type of trap could he set up this quick with only a knife on his person?" voiced Sergent Malenkov.

"Who knows what kind of ambush these Finns can dream up anyway?" replied Rykov.

This immediately sent a ripple of fear through the group as they looked around uneasily. Rykov immediately realized his mistake, knowing he had slowed the search as everyone was going to be looking over his shoulder, expecting the worst to happen.

Rykov, trying to rectify his mistake, said, "Oh, he probably thinks we aren't smart enough or good enough to be able to track him down. You know how egotistic these Finns are about their own abilities."

It didn't do much to lessen the fears of the group. The seed had been planted.

Vilho reached the first in a series of lakes by late afternoon. He had formulated a possible plan to lose his pursuers but he had to set the stage first. He wished the days weren't so long, but summer in these latitudes made for short nights and long days.

He waded into the water of several lakes to make them work at finding his trail. He hoped it would delay them long enough for darkness to set in. They would have to resume their search in the morning when his scent trail would be cold. It wasn't good to start the long evasion process in the dark. The first step demanded a good night's rest before he started on the second leg. Wading a small feeder stream entering a lake would make the search harder. He waded around the lake following the shoreline. Its sandy bottom made wading easy. He knew the Russians would stop for the night when they found where he had entered the stream. They would find remnants of his tracks in the sandy bottom, but that was what he wanted them to find.

At the far end of the lake, he came to the outlet stream and a blown down spruce suitable for his exit. In the middle of a grove of spruce trees, he found a place to camp making him invisible from the other end of the lake.

A wooden spear from a tree sapling served well to get trout from the stream for his supper. He built a small fire to cook the fish, lamenting that he had no salt to season it.

Vilho raked a pile of dead leaves under the blown down spruce and crawled in it like a hibernating bear. It was essential he get all the rest he needed in order to survive.

The Russians, predictable as ever, decided to make camp where Vilho entered the stream. Vilho chose his entry well as this was an excellent camp site. Rykov, dead tired from the unaccustomed exercise, gave the order to camp for the night.

The grey dawn and chattering of waking birds aroused Vilho from his nest. He washed in the stream and ate two more fish for breakfast. Two more he cooked, then wrapped in leaves to carry in his pocket to eat later.

Moving down the outlet stream, he looked for a small log he could carry, finding one near the stream entrance to the chain of lakes. The plan was to use the log to float down the lake. He need not have hurried as it was late afternoon before the men and dogs tracked him to the lake. It would take two to three days for them to find his trail if it didn't rain. They would have to traverse the lake going through a thick swamp bordering the lake. They wouldn't dare pass up any of it as they wouldn't know where he left the lake. They split the group to cover both shores making sure they didn't miss his exit.

Rykov had enough of trailing this man through the wilderness. The swamp around the lake was more than he wanted to travel. Three men went with him as he headed back to base. Before he left, he directed the rest of the crew to continue the search. Rykov was silent all the way back to camp as he tried to think of ways to explain this latest fiasco to Golovin in Helsinki. Thoughts of not reporting it came to mind. The news would get back to Golovin, and he would be in deeper trouble.

"Looks like a cloud build up in the west with some rain in the offing. This will obliterate my scent entirely. It's a long trek to the cabin. If rains don't come, I'll have to divert to another area," Vilho mused.

The rains did come two days later. The Russians had traversed the swamp to the other end of the lake. They emerged tired, covered with scratches from climbing under, over and through fallen trees. They were a bedraggled crew, covered with mud, mosquito bites, and mad at the world.

The rain made it impossible to track Vilho further. The officers ordered a return to base camp. The crew rejoiced, they had enough of chasing Vilho. They were looking forward to some hot food, clean clothes, and soft, dry beds.

Vilho knew the search would end at least temporarily, so he proceeded on to the Jonas cabin.

Chapter Six

Sweet Revenge

VILHO MADE IT TO THE CABIN but brooded about Mary being in town by herself. He thought the Russians might somehow take revenge on her. He knew she wasn't feeling herself since the rape by a Russian officer. These two things made him get up the next morning and head for town even though he was taking a tremendous risk.

On the trip he thought of Mary, his sweetheart for several years. She was in many ways his opposite. She was blonde, thin—almost too thin—and fair skinned, with an even temperament to go along with her classic beauty. Vilho had a fiery temper, which Mary tried to control with very little success.

They almost broke up because of the rape by the Russian officer. She felt dirty and suffered considerable anguish because of the event. Vilho convinced her that it wasn't her fault and that he felt no less love for her. This was an event over which she had no control.

Vilho arrived on the edge of town in mid afternoon. He sat hidden, watching her house to make sure the Russians had not formulated a trap for him. No one was around, so he slipped out of the woods after dark and into Mary's arms.

"Mary, we don't have much time. Pack everything you need in these two packs. Keep it light. We're going to go to see the Reverend Koski the first thing in the morning, get married and go to Jonas' cabin."

"Oh, Vilho, I want to . . . but are you sure after what happened to me?"

"I'm sure. I told you that before and that it was not your fault. I love you. That's all that matters."

They hurried and packed. Vilho felt uneasy in town thinking the Russians might show up any minute. It was a nice moonlit night so they walked to Reverend Koski's house. They sat down at the edge of the clearing near his house to await daylight.

Mrs. Koski answered their soft knock, recognized them and let them in. She whispered, "What are you two doing here at this hour of the morning?"

"We want to get married and go back into the wilderness. The Russians found out that I killed the men that killed Crazy Jake."

Mrs. Koski never blinked an eye. Everyone in town had liked Crazy Jake. "I'll get my husband, then fetch the neighbors as witnesses. First I need to fix us all some breakfast."

"No need. We're in a hurry."

"There's time for breakfast. Mary, you go fetch the neighbors while I cook."

Vilho fidgeted and paced the room, worrying about the Russians.

The neighbors came, and they all sat down to breakfast. Vilho bolted his portion down, but he had to wait for the rest of them. They finally got around to the ceremony.

Vilho thanked everyone and grabbed Mary by the arm so there wouldn't be any more delays and headed for the cabin.

The remote cabin, coupled with time together, made great strides in Mary's recovery from the rape. She worried at first that she might be pregnant. Such was not the case. This, in itself, was a great step in getting her thinking back to normal.

"Oh, Vilho, I'm so glad I don't have to bear that monster's child. I probably would have killed myself rather than bring his child into the world. I know I would have felt less love for the child, and it would have sensed it."

"I'm glad, too. We can get on with our own life. Let's have a baby of our own as soon as possible. I was so happy for Emma and Jonas, having a child on the way."

"I was too," Mary said. "She looked so radiant. I couldn't help be envious of her. I'm ready to try for our baby whenever you are."

Vilho picked her up gently and carried her to bed.

The next morning both were more loving than usual. Vilho felt content that he was on the way to becoming a father. Mary shared the same feeling.

Mary bustled about the kitchen humming happy nursery tunes. She remembered her own happy childhood and the way her mother sang her to sleep at night. Tears sprang to her eyes in remembrance of those happy times.

"I hope our time together will be as happy," she said under her breath.

A few days later Vilho said, "I feel I should get back to Kiivijarvi and the movement. There's so much that needs to be done, but I hate leaving you here alone. I'd take you along, but it's too dangerous."

"I'll be all right. I feel safe here now. This place has become a real safe haven of happiness for me."

Kiivijarvi was a training post for Finnish draftees and a supply base for smaller outposts surrounding the area. The killing of their commanding officer by Jonas Kekola interrupted their entire routine. They took him prisoner. He escaped and continually harassed the Russians. Word trickled back to the tsar in St. Petersburg, creating an urgency in tracking down and killing Jonas.

This resulted in the Finnish people thinking: if one man could do all this, then more effort on their part might drive the Russians out.

"I know, you have to go," Mary said. "I feel safe here and I'm not as anxious as I was at first. I wouldn't feel nearly as safe in town."

Vilho packed up the next morning and set out for town. He was ever on the alert as patrols were out looking for both him and Jonas.

His first stop was at the Lehtinen house in Kiivijarvi. He wanted to see if there was any news of Jonas and Emma in America and find out the latest about the Russians in the area.

He waited until dark to ease up to the house. Anna and Toivo were glad to see him and quickly brought him up to date on his best friend in America and the latest Russian news.

Anna said, "Emma and Jonas had a baby boy in America. They named it Vilho in your honor."

"I'm honored," said Vilho proudly. "I can't wait to get back to tell Mary the good news."

"They have a small farm in Northern Michigan. Jonas writes that the weather is very similar to ours, and the hunting and fishing is great. They are very much at peace."

"I'm happy for them. I need to see Mika at the Boar's Head. Do you suppose I could get Matt to go there and ask Mika to leave the back door to the store room open so I could sneak in?"

"I'm sure he'll do it. He should be home soon."

Matt came in shortly, and Vilho asked him to go to the Boar's Head.

He said, "I'm glad to do it. Why don't we go together? You could go around the back while I go in the front and tell Mika you'll be at the door."

"I don't see anything wrong with that unless they catch you and me together. You could be in big trouble."

"I don't care. It's dark and there's not much chance anyone will recognize us."

Vilho waited a few minutes at the store room door before Mika slipped it open and said, "Come on in, good friend, before someone sees you."

Once inside Mika clapped Vilho on the back saying, "I've been worried with so many Russians after you. We've heard rumors of your capture many times. Also I've missed you and your good fishing haunts."

"I have missed you too."

Mika acted as a clearing house for information. He served as the dispenser of needed funds as well. It was easy for him to give extra change to resistance people paying their check.

"Well, old man what do you need today?" asked Mika.

"I was wondering if you found out anything about the man that raped Mary from her description?"

"I thought that might be on your mind, and yes, I did find out what you need. The collar emblem Mary described is an Engineer emblem. The emblem and the fact the man was a full colonel boils it down to only one man, Yuri Tokarev. He's here on a survey to see if it's feasible to enlarge this operation. From what I've found out, he's not going to be here much longer. It looks like his work is about done, and he is recommending expansion of the operation. He may come back when and if they do decide to get bigger. Right now it's only a preliminary survey."

"I planned on going back tomorrow, but if I'm going to miss a chance at Yuri, I might stay over. Think you can find out anything more tonight?"

"I might, several of the regulars from the post come in and talk. I pick up stuff."

"I'll take a chance on you learning something more, but I have to get back to Mary soon."

"Here's a key to my apartment upstairs. Lock the door after you. I'll come up after a while if I find out anything significant."

Vilho eased out the store room door and up the back stairs to Mika's apartment. Mika left a small light burning so Vilho eased around to pull down the shades.

He turned up the light and lit two more lamps before sitting down in one of Mika's overstuffed chairs. He blew out a breath of air as he looked over Mika's living quarters. It was just like

Mika, big roomy with soft comfortable furniture, simplicity in itself, very lived in. Very much a living place for a man.

Vilho dozed and woke with a start with Mika standing over him.

"Vilho, you must have felt secure in my place to go to sleep like that. You were really out of it."

"I was tired. Too much constant tension here in town."

"I brought you a small steak and a bottle of wine. I've missed feeding you."

"It looks good. I'm really hungry all of a sudden."

"Sit and eat while I talk. You don't have much time to do anything about Yuri. He's leaving with the supply wagons next week. I don't know how you can get to him here as he seldom leaves the post. He probably knows someone may try to get back at him for the rape. I doubt that he knows you and Mary are connected. I would suggest you forget it, but I know you won't do that. My next suggestion would be to get him on the road to Helsinki."

"That might be a good idea."

"I've thought of a plan you might consider. The wagons rarely leave here early, so they usually stop for the first night at an abandoned farm about fifteen miles from here. There won't be many men with the group. If you get there early, you might be able to figure some way to surprise your man."

"When do they leave?"

"Next week on Wednesday."

"I'll be there. Just where is this farm where they stop?"

"It's easy to find. It's the only abandoned farm on the right about fifteen miles from here. The house is boarded up, but the barn is open so the men and horses usually spend the night in there."

"I'll come back next week and go down there early to scout the area. When they show up I'll be ready for them. I would appreciate you keeping tabs on Yuri and the trip. I'll check in with the Lehtinens and come here with Matt the same way we did today."

Vilho waited quietly in the dark. Mika told Matt what was happening, and Vilho gave him the essential details of his meeting with Mika as they walked back.

Vilho packed the supplies Toivo picked up for him while he was visiting Mika. He spent a restless night and was up before daylight, ready to head back.

Anna forced him to delay long enough to have breakfast. He bolted it down and was gone before the first grey light of dawn.

Mary was overjoyed to see him and chattered like a magpie about everything she had been doing.

Vilho said, "Slow down, Mary, so I can get a word in. I have lots of things to tell you. I talked to Mika. He told me about the man that raped you. His name is Yuri Tokarev, and he's an engineer on temporary duty here. He's leaving next week for Helsinki. If I'm to do anything about him, I'll have to do it soon."

"Oh, Vilho, I wish you wouldn't do anything. The deed is done, and there's no way to undo it."

"I want to make sure he doesn't get the chance to do the same thing to some other Finnish woman."

"But there's still a lot of danger. There's already a price on your head. This will make it worse."

"I feel like Jonas. They have to catch me first. We can't let the Russians get away with treating us like we're less than human."

"I realize that but I still worry about you, especially you and your fiery temper getting you into trouble you can't handle."

"Don't worry, I'll take care of myself. I promise not to do anything foolish."

Vilho did not elaborate on anything else he had in mind for Yuri. There was no point in upsetting Mary further.

For the next few days, they stayed close to the cabin, enjoying each other's company.

Mary didn't voice her fear of what might happen to Vilho if he went after Yuri. She was sure in her own mind that was exactly what he was going to do.

74

On Monday morning, Vilho started packing his rucksack. Mary interrupted him. "Are you really going to go after him?" "I don't know yet. If the opportunity comes up, I may do something, but I don't know for sure. I really need to go in and do some checking on the movement. We're thinking about moving into some other areas. Some of our people who took training with us were transferred. They would make a good cadre to start some resistance in their new locations. We need to give them additional training, money, and weapons. I have to see what we can do about it."

"I know you're trying to relieve my mind, and I appreciate it, but I still worry."

Vilho finished packing, kissed Mary goodbye and was on his way. The trip into Kiivijarvi was uneventful. He still took all the precautions of the hard-hunted animal.

He waited for darkness on the hill overlooking town so he could slip into the Lehtinen house unseen. A slight breeze made the wait very pleasant. He watched the darkness take hold and the road traffic dwindle to nothing. He eased on down, very much on the alert, to knock on the Lehtinen back door.

Matt opened the door and quickly pulled him inside, shutting the door with the same quick motion.

"Take care, Vilho, the Russians were here snooping around this afternoon. I doubt if they'll be back soon, but you never know."

"Well, let's not dally here, then. Let's get down to the Boar's Head and Mika. Here's a list of supplies and some money. No hurry on these. I'll be back in three or four days."

Matt and Vilho slipped quietly through the semi-deserted streets to the Boar's Head. Vilho went around to the back while Matt entered to let Mika know Vilho was out back.

Mika saw Matt, nodded his head in understanding and headed for the storeroom to open the door for Vilho.

As soon as Vilho stepped inside, Mika said, "Everything looks good, my friend. It looks like it's a go for Wednesday."

"That's good. I'll plan on leaving early in the morning to be there a day ahead to scout the place thoroughly."

"Why not bunk here for the night? I'll even give up my bed."

"I appreciate that, but the couch will do just fine. It looked soft and comfortable."

Mika gave Vilho the key to the upstairs and went back into the restaurant.

Mika came up later with a plate of the night's special, baked salmon.

"Mika, you didn't need to do that but it sure looks good. I know from your previous repasts of fish that it'll be superb."

"Not as good as our fresh-caught trout though."

"Yes, that's pretty hard to beat."

"I'll be back up later. I'll bring a bottle of wine, and we can talk if you don't fall asleep."

Mika did keep his word, and Vilho didn't fall asleep. They talked for several hours about the resistance movement and how to expand it all over Finland.

Vilho slept fitfully for several hours. He woke with the night turning from black to grey and was anxious to get out of town before anyone stirred. He dressed quickly and left a note for Mika, who was snoring peacefully in his bed.

Vilho slipped out of town as the sun turned the sky a dirty grey. It was too early for anyone else to be about. Once clear of town, he breathed a bit easier.

The farm was easy to find following Mika's directions. He reached the area well before noon.

He commented to himself. "I'll have plenty of time to make a plan of action between now and tomorrow night."

It was a small farm, the end of someone's dream. The house was boarded up. The barn was open with the main door hanging askew. Inside in one corner was some hay left over from the past. It was obvious the soldiers used it for comfort sleeping as there were several depressions in the hay about body size.

Vilho said under his breath, "I wonder why they never bothered to pry some boards off the door or windows and use the house for shelter? I'll check it out."

He looked around for something to pry boards loose, settling for a short iron bar.

He pried several boards loose from the door. He cringed with the sound of squeaking nails even though he knew there was no one around to hear it.

The door hadn't been opened for quite some time. The brute force of his shoulder made it give way grudgingly.

Inside, it was dark and musty. A few streaks of light came through the boarded up windows showing dust motes floating in the shafts of sunlight. Most of the furniture was still there. He wandered through the house in the dim light. Thoughts came to him of hiding in the house until the wagons came. The idea of being cooped up in the house didn't appeal to him.

Boarding the house back up, he looked for a more suitable place to spend the night. The barn and its soft hay would do just fine. He first scouted around the barn and the woods directly behind it. He wanted to make sure he had a rear exit and escape route in case the detail came sooner than expected.

While reconnoitering the woods, he built a small fire to fix himself a hot meal from items in his rucksack. No point in tipping his presence by the remains of a fresh fire near the barn.

After eating he went back to the barn, spread his bed roll in the hay and was soon fast asleep.

Sunlight streaming through the many loose boards on the barn woke him up. Picking up his bedroll and rucksack he retired to the patch of woods behind the barn to wait. A cold breakfast of roast beef and bread, given him by Mika the night before, stopped his hunger pangs.

The day dragged. Vilho watched the many birds and animals going about their daily chores. A few looked with curiosity at this new lump in their territory. One squirrel came within a few feet and decided he was nothing harmful and went about its business.

Late afternoon the wagons showed up, and Yuri was with them. He wasn't hard to recognize, dressed in the splendor of his dress uniform, shiny black boots, and spiked helmet in contrast to the drab working clothes of the other men.

Vilho watched them for a while, his anger mounting, thinking of what this man had done to his beloved Mary.

"You're going to pay dearly for your deed," muttered Vilho under his breath.

The men unhitched the horses, took off the harnesses and turned the teams loose with hobbles to crop the lush green grass of the field.

The men made preparations for cooking a meal and bedding down for the night. Several men gathered wood, making Vilho move further into the forest to avoid detection.

He watched as they bedded down, noting where Yuri settled to spend the night. No feasible plan came to him. The men were sleeping too close together to allow him to slip into the barn, kill Yuri and slip out undetected.

An hour passed by before Vilho thought it safe to leave the protection of the trees and draw closer to the barn. Still no plan would come to him.

Leaning up against the barn wall, he could hear snoring inside. It was frustrating to think the man he wanted was within his grasp but he could do nothing about it. He thought about rushing in, stabbing Yuri and rushing out to escape in the confusion. He thought about shooting him from a short distance away and then running for safety.

While he pondered all the different plans, he heard stirring in the hay. Peeking through a crack he thought he saw Yuri sitting up in his bed. He threw the cover off, slipped on his boots and got up.

The thought sprang to mind that Yuri was getting up to relieve himself. He eased closer to the door where he would come out if that was what he was going to do.

Yuri stepped from the barn a few feet from Vilho with his back to him. He was relieving himself. Vilho stepped forward two steps, drawing his knife. A swift thrust into the kidney and Yuri buckled slowly to the ground. The pain of that kind of wound was so terrible that Yuri uttered no sound.

Vilho rolled him over on his back, got down on one knee and hissed, "This is for raping my wife. I'm sending you to hell."

Hearing those words, Yuri's eyes flew wide open. Vilho thrust his knife directly into his heart, and Yuri knew no more. Vilho ripped open the front of the man's under clothing to write on his chest with his knife, "I, Vilho, killed him for raping my woman."

Melting into the forest, he blended with the dark of night. He got back on the road to town knowing full well that no one would be about that late. It might even be hours before Yuri's body was discovered. Rather than go into town, Vilho took a short cut through the forest toward the cabin. It was slow going, following the stars for direction in the black of the forest.

Daylight found him close to the cabin. He was anxious to see his Mary. At the clearing edge he gave the customary bird whistle to let Mary know he was coming.

Mary heard the familiar call and met Vilho half way in the clearing. After they kissed and hugged she said. "I was so worried about you. I knew you were going after that man, and my mind conjured up all kinds of mishaps."

"I'm all right. Not to worry. I'm here to stay for a while. You don't have to worry about your rapist. He is no more. Don't ask me for details."

"I won't, the deed is done. I know you felt you had to do it to keep him from getting someone else. I have a hard time condoning the killing. I suppose it's a woman's way."

With that they walked arm in arm back to the cabin.

Chapter Seven

Canoe

VILHO LAY DAY DREAMING ONE COLD MORNING, thinking of all the ways he could torment the Russians.

His thoughts strayed to a book with pictures of the American Indians and how they built canoes from the bark of the birch tree. Remembering the picture, the vision came to him that it would be easy enough to build one.

The forest grew the birch trees, and he could get pitch from the spruce. Willow and cedar could make the frame work. "It can't be that difficult. Besides, I need something to do," said Vilho to himself.

He built the canoe in his mind. When he had the idea fully visualized, he rose to cook breakfast for himself as he wanted to let Mary sleep. Anxious to get started on his project, he bolted down his breakfast and wrote Mary a note.

Outside there was a soft snow drifting down that would likely last for days.

Vilho nodded with satisfaction saying, "The weather's good for me to go out. The snow will fill my tracks quickly. The Russians won't go out on a day like this for the same reason."

He donned his skis, still thinking about his project.

"Cedar will do for the keel but I'll need some willow or ash that will bend easily for the ribs."

His mind sorted through the different areas he would have to visit to get all his materials.

"I remember a swamp where I saw a small cedar with a bend at the base that would do for the keel. The end will save me a lot of saw and ax work to get it into the right shape."

He found the tree quickly. After cutting it down, he smeared mud over the fresh cut so it would not be noticeable.

He dragged the tree, branches and all, back to the cabin as he didn't want to leave any visible signs of his being there. The tree pulled easily on the new snow.

The keel went well. He used ax and saw to shape it, burning the debris as he went. He loved the smell of the aromatic cedar as he worked. The cedar helped clear some of the mustiness from the cabin. Mary tried to help but he shooed her away saying, "Right now you're in the way. Later, I'll need your help. This is almost as good as a sauna with the extra heat from burning the chips, the smell of cedar and me sweating. It all makes me feel good."

The next day he went to the creek bottom to gather willow for the framework. He wasn't sure how much he was going to need, so he gathered a great pile of it, binding it with other pieces of slender willow. This great mountain of willow, he hoisted on his back and hauled it back to the cabin.

"I don't know how the Indians formed their frames, but I remember fishermen weaving fish traps from willow. I think that basic method will do."

The willow strips ran through the keel and then back onto itself coming to a taper at both ends. It worked out well. Now the job of covering it would begin. Mary was a big help in weaving the willow.

"Tomorrow I'll look for birch bark and spruce pitch, but tonight I'm going to sleep."

"You do look tired. I'll fix you something to eat before you go to bed."

Vilho woke the next morning wondering vaguely why his hands were so sore. Then he remembered his willow weaving. This prompted him to get an early start gathering the rest of the materials needed.

"I wonder where I can get birch bark without leaving obvious signs for the Russians. The small island on Lake Jarvi has both birch and spruce. It's not big enough to warrant a search but it does have the trees I need. I'll get my skis and head for there right now."

He cut the bark from the tree in partial pieces so it wouldn't kill the tree. He cut close to the ground and on trees in clumps so the cutting would not be obvious. This, in the off chance that someone did come to the island. He rolled the bark into tubes much like it had been when on the tree.

Spruce gum was his next material to gather. Sap seeped through the bark and coagulated into hard, amber nuggets. Prying them loose with his knife, he filled his rucksack. If he needed more, he knew he could gather this material anytime. Shouldering his load of birch bark and spruce gum, he headed for home.

It stopped snowing an hour after he returned to the cabin. This worried him as he knew the Russian patrols would be out soon and might find his trail. He looked at his recent ski tracks to discover they weren't completely covered.

"All I can hope is that it snowed long enough to cover my tracks further out. I made them a little longer ago and they might be covered. I know the Russians are due to swing by this way soon. I hope it isn't until after the next storm."

"Oh, Vilho, I hope you aren't taking too many chances on this project," Mary said.

"Don't worry. I think my tracks are covered well enough. I like this idea of using the canoe to harass the Russians some more."

His canoe work slowed as he didn't dare have a fire during daylight hours, fearing a patrol might see the smoke. He did fit the bark to the canoe and laced it with rawhide.

Vilho was impatient, wanting to get back to work on his project. He calmed down, reminding himself it would be two months until spring melted lakes and streams so that he could try out the canoe.

The weather turned and started snowing. Vilho gave a sigh of relief knowing that the Russians hadn't found his tracks and he could get back to his project.

The snow turned into a howling blizzard. He knew the patrols wouldn't be out, for which he was thankful. A hot fire was needed to melt the spruce pitch. He turned the canoe this way and that to pour pitch into all the seams. Rawhide was coated with pitch so it wouldn't get wet and loosen.

Standing back, looking at his finished project he said, "Well, I guess I'll have to wait until spring to see if it will hold water."

He and Mary sat admiring their handiwork. Mary was glad the mess was over and she could finally clean up the cabin.

He said, "I can think of many ways we can use it to fish remote areas and as a getaway."

A thought came to him as he sat there, "Why not fill it with water here to see if it leaks. I would hate to be out on a lake and find out that I'm taking on water."

After many trips to his small spring, he had the canoe full, with not one single leak showing up.

Vilho looked at the canoe full of water and said, "It's a shame to waste all that water."

They heated several buckets of water from the canoe until the water was warm. They stripped to the buff and had a first class bath, laughing and splashing each other and getting the floor soaked.

"I was going to scrub the floor anyway so this makes it easy," said Mary, not at all perturbed by the mess. "It's all soaped up and ready to scrub," said Mary, laughing with glee.

They rinsed the canoe out and set it to dry, impatiently awaiting a trial run in the spring.

Spring did come in all its glory. The melting snow showed bare spots with grass starting to turn green even with snow on the ground elsewhere. Soon flowers sprouted in profusion. The buds on the trees swelled and burst forth with tiny, pale green shoots. The shoots would soon burst into leaves. Birds were busy building nests in every tree and bush. The profusion of life renewing itself abounded throughout the forest. Vilho and Mary felt renewed and full of promise of better things to come for them both.

Vilho whittled paddles for the canoe. He thought long and hard about where to launch their prize.

"There's lots of lakes I'd like to fish, but I have to think of this as part of our escape planning."

One lake came to mind in a chain of lakes. He had always wanted to fish the other side but the walk around from the chain side seemed too much effort. With the canoe it would be easy.

He and Mary had a hard time getting the canoe down the narrow track from the cabin to the lake. A small stream, swollen by spring run off, saved them several miles of portaging. This also gave him a chance to try out his canoe in shallow water.

"It works fine, Mary. Get in. We'll go for a ride to test it out and see if it works."

"No, you go on. I'm afraid it will tip over out there and dump me in that ice-cold water."

"All right. I'll try it out myself."

With only a short portage, he was soon in the water and fishing. Everything went fine until he had a sizeable strike. He pulled too hard, toppling over backwards out of the canoe. Up he came, gasping and sputtering from the icy water. Mary laughed until she thought was going to fall in too.

"Don't laugh, or I'll tip the canoe and put you in. I'm freezing. I can't get back in the canoe out here without dumping it again. I'll have to push it to shore."

He pushed the canoe to shore and built a fire to dry his clothes. He'd be more careful in the future. He was satisfied with the canoe, despite the dunking.

He had mixed emotions about where to leave the canoe. He wanted it close so he could use it for fishing. If he used it to escape the Russians they would concentrate their search efforts too close to the cabin. He pondered the dilema for a minute, but harrasing the Russians won out.

The decision was to move it further away. They hid the canoe in some brush and went back to the cabin.

"I'm going to go alone this time, Mary. You'll be all right for a few days. I'll take some supplies, and I'll get some fish along the way and bring some home. This will be a pretty hard trip."

The journey took three days. Vilho took his time, thoroughly enjoying his new toy. He explored, fished and camped early. He scouted the shore area of the land so he would know how it lay in relation to the water. He couldn't believe the freedom the canoe gave him and the ease of portaging it through the chain of lakes. The canoe was so light, it and his supplies were easily portable from one area to another. He thought of escape in the same manner. He could leave the Russians diligently searching one area, while he was miles away, laughing at them.

The trip convinced him to give it the ultimate test. Give the Russians a few miserable days hunting for him without success.

In the past he had never deliberately set out to have them chase him. This time he was confident he could escape to really frustrate them.

The more he thought about it, the more he liked the idea. The plan flowed easily through his mind.

Russian mentality was such that he could predict accurately what they would do under a given set of circumstances. They were predictable to the point of being ridiculous.

At first he was going to wait for warmer weather when it would be a bit more tolerable for himself. After thinking about it, he opted for a more immediate plan.

"I can elude them, be back snug in the cabin with Mary while they spend several wet, cold, miserable days and nights out here looking for me."

Sinking the canoe in a small stream, he headed back to the cabin. He needed to get supplies and lay the trap for the Russians in the area of the canoe. On his way out, he noted land marks that he could recognize in the dark.

Chuckling to himself, he thought of all the misery he was going to subject the Russians to on this outing.

Vilho timed his return to the area to coincide with the Russian search pattern.

A week's supply of food in his rucksack, in case the Russians changed the search pattern due to weather. The Russians didn't go out in bad weather. The storm destroyed all sign and odor for the dogs.

A small hill overlooking the valley was his observation post. Experience with their grid pattern told him they would use it to get to their starting point. From this point he could see them a long way off. The Russians would get a good look at him before he went for the safety of the swamp.

The Cossacks wouldn't follow him on foot into the swamp, and the horses couldn't negotiate it. It was beneath their dignity to dismount and act as foot soldiers. They would stand and wait for the foot soldiers and dogs to come up from the rear and go into the swamp.

This would suit Vilho just fine. He wanted them to follow closely so he could perpetuate the ghost theory.

He didn't have long to wait. They were as predictable as sunrise. He knew they were coming long before he saw or heard them. The imperceptible change in forest sounds told him something was happening. Long association with the forest made him rely on the forest creatures' senses more than his own.

The Cossacks came over the hill with their horses at a walk, the infantry and dogs trailing behind. They weren't alert. The search pattern starting point, was still further down the valley.

Vilho roused himself from his sitting position, lazily starting his walk down the hill. He watched from the corner of his eye acting as though he didn't see the troop, as if anyone could possibly miss seeing them.

One of the troopers whooped as he saw Vilho. He started at full gallop, wanting to be the first one there. The rest of the troop broke ranks to follow.

Vilho turned his head as though he saw them for the first time. He acted frightened as he turned, running for the swamp, he reached his goal with time to spare. The Cossacks fired a few shots at him in frustration. He could hear the bullets thudding into trees behind him. The shots hurried the infantry and dogs.

He eased over to the small stream where he had sunk the canoe. With ample time to spare, he removed the rocks, tipping the canoe on its side to empty the water. Loading his gear carefully, he pushed off, making a few paddle swirls to cover any skid marks of the canoe. He wanted them to think he swam across to the other side.

This would make them go around the chain of lakes four or five miles to get to the other side. He was reasonably sure they would go around to the west as it was almost double the distance to go around the east side. East was the direction Vilho took.

Vilho rounded a point near his original entry. Beaching the canoe, he climbed a small hill to watch the antics of his pursuers.

The dogs tracked unerringly to the edge of the lake. Vilho watched in amusement as the Russians stood there shouting, waving their arms and pointing at the other side of the lake. He knew just what was happening and what they were saying.

The dog handlers went up and down the shore for some distance to make sure he hadn't doubled back on the same side. When they were sure this was not the case, they sent a runner back to inform the Cossacks. They started wending their way to the other side to see if they could pick up his tracks.

Vilho smiled to himself as he slipped down the hill to his canoe. He kept the hill between himself and the Russians.

The Russians could have gone a half mile from the lake to high ground. They chose to follow the lake shore, fighting swarms of mosquitos and climbing over blown down trees, and stumbling on moss-covered rocks.

It was dark before they got around to the other side to meet the Cossacks who had an easy ride around. They made camp and spent a miserable night fighting mosquitos. They resumed the search at daylight but found no sign of Vilho. The ghost rumors persisted.

Vilho made a leisurely trip up the lake to another stream where he sank the canoe. He walked back to the cabin. The Russians spent several futile days looking for his tracks on the wrong side of the lake.

All snug in the cabin with his wife, Vilho couldn't help laughing at the plight of the Russians. He knew from experience they would concentrate their effort in that same area for weeks.

Mary voiced concern, "Vilho, you enjoy tormenting the Russians too much. I worry about you carrying this game of yours too far and getting caught."

"The Russians have no idea what I'm doing. It's true I do enjoy tormenting them. The more time they spend chasing me the less time they will have to harass the people in town. I'll give them a little time and more frustration, before I do it to them again."

Vilho sat by the fire planning his next move against the Russians. He wanted to make their life as miserable as possible, especially those who wanted to kill him. He wished he could get some of the higher ranking officers out on the searches to make life miserable for them as well.

One particular place came to mind where there was a lot of stagnant water and an excellent breeding place for mosquitos. It had many blown down trees making walking and tracking extremely slow and difficult. This would give the mosquito population plenty of time to find the group and give them grief.

His plan entailed moving the canoe, but he thought it was worth it. Some mosquitos would find him but his scent trail would bring the mosquitos to await the coming of the Russians. They would be there in abundance when they came through at a much slower pace.

Back at Russian headquarters, the troops in on the chase were having a critique of their operation. The critique was one sided with Major Rykov doing most of the talking and yelling. Much of the controversy was about the theory that Vilho was a ghost. Rykov was livid with rage. He didn't believe in ghosts nor the theory that Vilho had supernatural powers to disappear at will. Some of his men weren't so sure. Most were uneducated and superstitious. They brought their beliefs with them into the army.

The men were impatient to get cleaned up from the swamp mud and grime they had endured for the past several days. They were all covered with bumps from mosquito attacks. Finally, Rykov dismissed all but the Cossack commander and the infantry commander.

Rykov started a blistering tirade aimed at the two commanders for letting Vilho slip through their fingers.

Toklat came back with, "We're not sure it was Vilho. We didn't get close enough to get a good look at him."

Rykov roared back, "If it wasn't Vilho, why did he run, and why did he lead you on a wild goose chase? On top of that, no one was supposed to be in the area without special permission. We haven't issued an entry permit for days!"

"Well, yes," conceded Toklat, "No one else could have given us the slip so easily."

"Bullshit, you people couldn't find your asses with both hands! I don't know what I'm going to have to do to get a crew together that can run this renegade to ground."

Toklat, ignoring the tirade, said, "I think we ought to concentrate our efforts in that area. When we first saw him, he wasn't aware that we were near. I don't think he would stray far from his hideout. I believe he's in that area somewhere."

"That's the only thing that makes sense out of the entire fiasco. We can double or triple the patrols in that area, but I think we ought to give it a few days rest to let him get complacent. I want routine patrols run for the next few days. Then we will hit the area in full force to see if we can catch him in the open. If not, we'll comb the area inch by inch to see if we can find his hideout and destroy it."

Operation Triple Search went into effect the next day. The triple patrol was hand picked and standing by while the routine patrols continued.

Vilho couldn't have asked for anything better to fit his plans for further harassment of the Russians.

Replenishing his supplies, he headed back to the area where he had hidden the canoe. He picked out another hill overlooking his escape route to the swamp. He built himself a small fire of dry twigs to cook himself a meal. From force of habit he built the fire small and of dry materials to create no smoke.

He laughed out loud saying, "I don't care this time if they do see my smoke. I'm trying to get them to chase me!"

After he finished his meal, he deliberately threw some green wood on the fire. It wouldn't be long before they would see the smoke and would come running. He cleaned all the forest debris away from the fire so it wouldn't get away if he had to leave in a hurry. He added more green wood, sending up a grayish black plume of smoke like a beckoning beacon.

Several miles away, Triple Force was moving into the area. The civilian population had been denied access, so that any tracks found should be those of Vilho.

The advance scouts saw the smoke first, signalling to the rest of the troops by hand signal and pointing ahead.

Toklat rode up to see what they were pointing at. "That has to be him, no permits were issued. If it's someone else, they're sure going to catch hell from me."

He waved the group to come up to him.

"Men," he said, "We think that might be Vilho's fire up ahead. I want all three troops spread out in a skirmish line with the infantry right behind. Each of the dog handlers will hang onto the stirrup of one of the troopers. That way they can get into tracking position as soon as possible. We'll proceed at a walk until we see him or are near the fire. Then proceed at full gallop to him or the fire site. The troopers with dog handlers come as fast as you can, we realize the handlers can't go at full gallop but do try to keep up. The infantry will proceed at double time into the tracking area. Try to stay as close to the mounted troops as possible. If he gets into heavy timber where the horses can't follow, I want the infantry there to chase him."

A few catcalls and jeers came from the infantry, and someone from the back made the comment, "Why don't you prima donna troopers get off your horses to give chase, or is that beneath your dignity?"

"Who said that?" shouted Toklat, "I'll have him horse whipped!"

Dead silence in the ranks. Toklat turned his back only to hear a few boos from the ranks. He turned, glowering but could do nothing.

The Cossack commander couldn't understand this as his group was all volunteer and would never question the commander on his tactics or orders.

"All right. Forward at a walk. Ho." commanded Toklat.

The "Ho" put two crows to flight, giving their usual alarm call. None of the troopers noticed, but Vilho picked it up. He brought his senses to a more alert status. Adrenalin flowed as he gathered his gear in preparation for flight. The forest sounds changed imperceptibly, jumping his own senses another step higher.

Vilho wouldn't admit, even to himself, how much he enjoyed the chase. It was the adrenalin high that was sustaining him. He didn't stop to analyze his own motives for making life miserable for the Russians. He kept telling himself it was patriotism, which was true, but he enjoyed the game immensely. It was very much a high-stakes game with his life in the balance.

The Russians came into view as Vilho started his slow walk toward the swamp. Again, he acted like he didn't see them until they started toward him at full gallop. When they started the gallop Vilho moved out in a long, easy run for the swamp. He was well into the swamp before they even got close. This time they didn't bother shooting at him.

Lieutenant Korsakov, one of the first Cossack officers there was trying to get the dog handlers and infantry to go on into the swamp after Vilho. It was utter confusion with men, horses, dogs, and their handlers milling around. Other men were shouting confusing orders with no one paying any attention.

Korsakov dismounted. Shouting at the top of their lungs, Korsakov and Toklat got the dog handlers on the right track with the infantry following close behind.

The Cossacks, still mounted, were looking with disgust at the whole melee. They wouldn't dismount to chase this phantom through the swamp. Horse and rider couldn't penetrate the heavy growth. The Cossacks weren't going to get separated from their horses under any circumstances.

Korsakov made the mistake of ordering camp made on the spot. A half mile up the hill, they would have avoided the hordes of mosquitos coming out of the swamp.

Vilho plunged into the swamp following his marked trail. Every few feet he would strip leaves to wipe his sweaty brow. He threw them off the trail to confuse the dogs. The handlers followed the dogs through rougher areas, helping delay the pursuit.

Vilho was making it as tough as possible for his pursuers. He walked on logs across bogs where he knew men with dogs couldn't follow. He traveled at a much faster pace than his pursuers, and, even then, the mosquitos found him. He didn't mind as this would concentrate the mosquito attack on the men behind him.

Vilho would really have laughed if he could have seen the chaos he created. The Russians were sweating, cursing and swatting at swarms of mosquitos. Vilho's false leads created a lot more confusion. Several times the dog handlers followed false leads, only to come back and start again. Black, oozy swamp mud covered everyone. Clothes and skin were torn by sharp brush and branches. The Russians were getting tired as they climbed over, under and through brush and trees that had fallen down over the years. Several of the infantry used the short sword of the cavalry and fared a little better as they could hack a pathway of sorts. Most of the others tried to follow the brush hackers, but progress was still slow. After six hours of fighting the futile battle against nature, Korsakov ordered them back from the swamp.

Vilho reached the canoe knowing the Russians were still far behind. He took his time to empty the rocks from the canoe and float it once more. He could hear the Russians faintly behind him. From the sounds he could tell there was a lot of miserable soldiers back there. He grinned, knowing his plan was working. He said to himself, "I wish the commandant was getting a taste of this misery. He will get his share of misery from Helsinki when he has to report another failure. I'm sure he's going to alter the facts as much as possible. It's still going to go down as another failure."

Vilho loaded his gear. Pushing the canoe out, he made sure he didn't leave any telltale canoe signs for the Russians to read. Footprints led them right to the water's edge. Paddling down the lake, smiling to himself, he said, "I have given you the slip once again."

He said out loud, "I would stay and watch you men in your misery, but there are too many of those pesky mosquitos to suit me. Goodbye!"

The Russians reached the lake shore only to discover Vilho's tracks leading into the water. They didn't know they were coming to a lake. It was not visible from their entry area. Several of the men had been on the chase when Vilho made his first canoe escape.

One of the men said, "That damn Finn swam across the lake, but did he swim up the lake or down. We'll never find where he got out. Last time we spent several miserable days looking for tracks and found none, I know he's a ghost."

Toklat ordered the men back out of the swamp after they were sure Vilho hadn't doubled back. The return trip was much worse. The mosquitos, now concentrated in the return pathway, attacked the soldiers viciously and unrelentingly. Several men, temporarily blinded by mosquito bites, needed help to get out. It was a tired, bedraggled group that staggered out of the swamp to the Cossack Camp.

The troops opted to stay there for the night. Neither commander had any idea where to continue their search, other than go to the other side of the lake in the morning.

The men in camp, cleaned up and fed, felt better. The happiness did not last. Mosquitos swarmed out of the swamp at dark, looking for fresh blood. The air hummed with mosquitos. The men cursed and slapped at the buzzing little monsters. Some got under covers but the pests still managed to find their targets. The insistent buzzing was almost worse under the confines of the covers.

Some of the men built small smudge fires of green grass. They fared a little better but only as long as they stayed in the choking smoke.

Vilho had a leisurely paddle up the lake. He took out some fish line and hooks, cut himself a willow pole and proceeded to catch some fish. He caught several trout for his supper.

Vilho picked a small stream entering the lake to stash his canoe for the third time.

He said to no one in particular. "I'm glad this works so well, it gives me one more emergency escape route."

A quick supper of trout cooked over dry wood tasted wonderful, but the mosquitos concentrated near the water. He bolted his food so he could leave the area.

He took a circuitous route back to where he entered the swamp. He wanted to see if the troop was still there or if they had given up and gone home.

Vilho topped a rise overlooking the Russian camp just before dark. Already the men were fighting mosquitos. Vilho laid out his bedroll to spend the night. He was anxious to see how they fared camped that close to the swamp. It was working out even better than expected.

On his bluff, with a cooling breeze keeping the mosquitoes away, he remarked to himself, "Must be a couple of real green leaders. They should know better than to camp near a stagnant swamp at this time of year. This is going to be one miserable bunch of men by morning."

Vilho spent a comfortable night on his hilltop.

Morning found him looking down at a completely chaotic camp. He couldn't hear what they said but he could tell that they were miserable. He took out his telescope for a closer look. He was amazed how many men were temporarily blinded from mosquito bites. He felt sorry for them, but the leaders should have known better than to camp that low.

Vilho watched the harangue between officers and men. He could see they had a near mutiny on their hands. Officers and enlisted men packed up and headed back, too miserable to even continue the search.

Vilho waited until they were well out of sight before he crossed their path. Back at the cabin, he savored the misery he had put the Russians through, giving Mary all the details.

The near mutiny of their men prompted the two leaders to abandon the search and head back. They knew what Rykov was going to say, but they also didn't know how to cope with the near mutiny of their men.

So much for inexperienced woods people. If they had pitched their camp higher, they would have few mosquitos, if any. The breeze would have kept them cooler at the higher elevation as well. The men would have felt better, and they could have continued with the search.

Both commanders were going back to camp with a feeling of dread. They both knew the tirade they were going to have to endure from Rykov.

Korsakov wasn't worried as much as Toklat. He was under separate command and didn't have to answer to anyone but his own commander. The *Hetman* of his unit would be more sympathetic than Rykov, but it was still going to be an arduous ordeal.

Toklat broke the long silence by saying, "We better get our stories straight. That ogre back at headquarters will find some reason to have us horse whipped for not catching Vilho."

"I agree that we should have our stories straight, but no one is going to horse whip me, no matter what! We Cossacks, answer to no one but another Cossack. Rykov can order my commander to have me horsewhipped, but I doubt that my commander would do it."

"Well, I think we should stick to the truth that he gave us the slip by swimming across the lake. I wasn't on the last search when he swam the lake. I know they were looking for a needle in a hay stack. If we explain how far it was around the lake, and that we had only two days rations, we might get by with a stiff reprimand."

"I'm not counting on it," replied Korsakov.

"Neither am I," rejoined Toklat, "I don't know how we could have held this rag-tag bunch together on short rations and shorter tempers."

"Speak for your own rag-tag bunch. We Cossacks, have proper discipline."

This really hurt Toklat, and he retorted in kind, "Then why didn't your well-disciplined group stay behind and hunt Vilho down without us? Your group said you would run Jonas to ground in a couple of weeks. Here it is a year later and you're still chasing him. Now we got another one. We're not a bit closer to catching either of them."

"We haven't had much help from your men. Look at them. They're a mess."

"I would like to know what your men would look like if they had dismounted and gone through that miserable swamp like my men did! Your people are too damn proud to get off their horses, and Vilho probably knows it. That's why he heads for heavy stuff every time. He knows that horse and rider can't follow!"

Korsakov had no answer because he knew it was true, but it infuriated him to have this failing pointed out to him.

They rode in silence the rest of the way back.

The two leaders were right about the tirade they had to face. Rykov was livid with rage when he heard they lost Vilho again.

"Why didn't you follow up by going to the other side of the lake?" he screamed, "You should have sent some men to the other side to look! So you had a bad night. You could have sent a rider back, and we would have sent you a relief column! Now it's too late to follow up."

Korsakov said, "It was your men that didn't want to go to the other side."

"Don't put the blame on someone else. I'm tired of this constant bickering and blame passing between commanders. No one will take the blame for failures."

Korsakov drew himself up to his full height, sucked in his stomach and said, "I'm a Cossack, and as such I'm not directly under your command. I don't have to take such abuse!"

Rykov reached into his desk drawer pulling out a dueling pistol. Cocking back the hammer, he pointed it directly at the head of Korsakov, saying quietly but in deadly earnest, "I'm the supreme commander of this area. I have full authority to do what ever is necessary to maintain discipline. Right now you are making mutinous sounds. One more such remark from you, and I'll blow your head off."

Korsakov blanched and said, "Yes sir."

The room was quiet.

Rykov put the pistol away and said, "Let's proceed."

They grew attentive after that episode. No one wanted to annoy him again. There was a rumor afloat that the major had killed a man under similar circumstances. This incident lent credence to the story.

The major began quietly, "I think we are right in our first assumption that Vilho is holed up somewhere in that area. This is the second time we've sighted him in that vicinity. We should concentrate our efforts there."

"Sir," Toklat said, "I think Vilho set this situation up to humiliate us. I don't think he is near that area at all."

"Captain, when I want comments from you people, I'll ask for them and not before!"

Toklat turned beet red, biting his lip to keep from trembling.

"We'll continue," said Rykov, "I said, before Toklat interrupted, we will concentrate our efforts in that area. I'm certain we will flush that renegade from his lair somewhere in that vicinity."

The two officers who came out of the area exchanged knowing looks, suggesting that the major was wrong but did not dare voice their opinions.

"We'll set up a base camp near the area," continued Rykov. "I want most of our force concentrated. We can spend more time on search patterns rather than traveling."

One of the other officers had the temerity to ask, "Won't Vilho vacate the area when he sees all the activity of a full blown camp?"

The major sighed, looking down his nose with chilling effect. "When I ask for your comments, it's the time to give them. For your information, we'll move several patrols into the area. It will be bottled up before we move in with our full camp."

Rykov finished his outline of the operation, asking for any comments or questions. No one dared voice an opinion.

"That's all, then. We'll put it together in the morning."

They all left. Once out of earshot of Rykov, they all voiced skepticism of the operation.

The move was made as per Rykov's orders, and the search continued in the area until fall. Cold weather and a late snow forced them back into town greatly frustrating Rykov with another failure.

Rykov made the comment, "I'm glad there's only one Jonas and only one Vilho or we would really be in big trouble back in St. Petersburg."

Little did he know there was a force coming to life with a lot more like Vilho to resist the Russian rule.

Rykov had one more problem. Korsakov reported the pistol incident to Captain Ustinov.

Ustinov stormed into Rykov's office, saying, "I command my men. You do not. You may outrank me, but I am not really under your command. Pull out your pistol and aim it at me, and I will make you eat it. If you think you can command me, try it. My unit will tear you apart limb from limb, and we will go back to Russia."

He strode out of the office before Rykov could reply.

Rykov sat there dumfounded for several minutes trying to regain his composure. No one had talked to him like that before. He knew Captain Ustinov meant every word.

Rykov said to himself, "I don't know what's happening. I can't get any respect or get any one to do anything right. I seem to be in trouble with everyone all the time. If I could capture even that damn Vilho, my life would right itself again."

Ustinov went back to his unit and called his troops in for a meeting.

When they all gathered in front of his quarters, he told them about the pistol incident between Korsakov and Rykov.

"I went to his office and told him there would be no more of those kind of happenings to my men. I told him we are a separate command. If anything like that happens again I want to be notified immediately. This does not mean you do not have to obey orders given by Rykov. It only means that the orders must be justified, and you, as my troopers, will not be humiliated in any way. Remember, we are soldiers first, but we do not have to take any humiliating treatment from anyone, ever. Any questions? None! Then dismissed."

Chapter Eight

Snow Blind

VILHO WOKE UP RESTLESS. Winter lay heavily around the small cabin in the forest, and he had been unable to get out much except to cut firewood. For an active man like Vilho, the need to do something more had been growing in him for some time. He wanted to work with the resistance movement but getting to town and back undetected in the heavy snow would be unlikely. He decided to go ice fishing.

"Its been a long time since we had any trout," he told Mary. "I remember this lake with lots of trout and a little, old, rickety cabin where I can spend the night."

Mary, well aware of his restlessness of late, offered encouragement. "Getting out will do you good. I've been wanting a nice trout to cook."

Gathering his fishing gear, his sheepskin-lined sleeping bag, Vilho packed his rucksack. Mary fixed some cold meat and bread in case the fish refused to bite. For bait, he took strips of raw venison. When he was soon to leave, Mary suddenly begged to go with him.

"It's too cold for you to go. This spring we'll go," said Vilho gently.

Mary pouted but knew it would not do any good to beg further. In her heart she knew Vilho needed this time alone.

Vilho thought about the tracks he would be leaving. According to the predictable Russian grid pattern, they wouldn't be in the area for quite some time, and the Russians seldom deviated from their master plan.

The woods were pleasant. It hadn't snowed lately so there wasn't any snow clinging to the trees. The sun came out bright and clear, making the snow glitter and sparkle like diamonds. The air felt soft and clean. It felt good to be alive.

I'm in no hurry to get there, Vilho thought, *so I can dawdle along at a leisurely pace and enjoy being outdoors. I'll fish today and possibly tomorrow morning if the cabin is in good enough shape to spend the night.*

The small lake and cabin was as he remembered it. The cabin sat in a grove of spruce trees, right on the shore of the lake. It was still in fair shape so he put his gear down, planning to spend the night.

He chopped some holes in the ice and laid out his lines so he could watch them while he cleaned the cabin and built a fire. This would be a pleasant interlude. In retrospect, he wished he had given more consideration to Mary's going. Surely she suffered cabin fever as much as he had. Having her with him would have been enjoyable. This cabin's not really comfortable, but Mary probably wouldn't have minded roughing it. Even as he thought this, however, he knew he was okay with a little time to himself. Cabin fever was like that.

Someone, a long time before, had built the small cabin by the lake. Surely not a residence, the log structure probably had served as a getaway and a fishing or hunting cabin. It had deteriorated over time but was still sound enough to be useable, though the inside smelled of rotting wood and mold. Vilho gave it a good sweeping with a brush broom to get rid of dirt, leaves, mouse droppings, and stale odors.

The fish were hungry and biting. Every few minutes, Vilho had to interrupt his house cleaning to take fish off the hook and bait the lines again again. He soon had a respectable number of trout laid out on the ice next to his holes. He had plenty of fish for a meal that night plus some extra to take home. His mouth watered at the prospect. Cold water trout tasted the best.

Darkness came early. Vilho picked up his lines and catch. He cleaned the fish outside the cabin, knowing that a mink or weasel would pick up the entrails to supplement their meager winter diets.

The cabin had no fireplace, stove, nor chimney. Vilho built a fire ring of rocks right in the middle of the dirt floor. He kept the door open to let out the smoke until the fire burned to coals. Small green sticks woven into a grid, made an excellent way to cook his fish. The trout went down with great relish.

He crawled into his sleeping bag early. The bed, composed of poles and spruce boughs he cut from the trees around the cabin would do for the night. The next day he planned to fish a bit more and then head back to the cabin.

He woke early to re-chop the holes that had frozen over in the night. He tended his lines and packed up at the same time, catching ten more fish in the process. Added to previous day's catch, he would have plenty for home. There might even be some extra to take into town on his next trip. Toivo dearly loved trout. The fish froze instantly when he laid them on the ice. He put them into his rucksack, gathered up the rest of his gear and headed for home.

He was thinking to himself how the fish froze so quickly that when he got home and put them into water they would come back to life. It was a silly thought, but he felt happier than he had in days. The outing had really done him a lot of good.

Shouts off in the distance jolted him back to reality. He was alert immediately. Standing stock still for a few minutes, he tried to locate the direction of the sounds. He pinpointed the sounds as coming from over the next hill. The shouts seemed odd, almost as if there were several people in distress. He couldn't make up his mind to run away or investigate the sounds. Curiosity got the best of him, and he decided to check out the situation.

They haven't seen me, he told himself. *There's no way they could know that I'm around whoever or whatever is making those sounds.*

Vilho moved toward the sounds keeping plenty of cover between him and the noise. When he reached the brow of the hill he looked on in amazement to see a Russian troop wandering around in circles. They were bumping into each other, trees and brush. They looked drunk—shouting, calling and cursing everyone and everything. Vilho watched them for a long time before the realization came to him that they were all snow blind.

Vilho continued to watch, trying to make up his mind what to do about the ridiculous situation. If it wasn't so serious, it would be fun to watch this comic opera, grown men going around and around doing everything wrong.

He wondered how long they had been like that. They must be raw recruits not to know they would need eye protection in the bright snow. They probably didn't think they needed them. He thought he should leave them there to die because they were his enemies. Then he got an inkling of an idea to make the situation work out for them and for them to think Jonas was still in the area.

He sat down on a nearby log to watch the soldiers. He knew they couldn't see him. The more he watched, the sorrier he felt for them. If not treated, they could remain blind, even if they managed to find their way out of the wilderness.

A definite plan came to mind, but he knew he must help them to make it work. He skied down to the nearest man. The man did not know he was near. Vilho commanded, "Stand still. Do not move!"

A bewildered look came over the soldier's face making Vilho realize that the man hadn't understand his Finnish. Vilho gave the command for attention in Russian. The soldier came to attention, standing ramrod stiff. Vilho repeated the command

103

until each soldier did the same thing. When he had them all standing still, he took them one at a time and sat them down on a fallen tree trunk. Once seated, he took ointment from his first aid kit and anointed their eyes. The one Russian officer finally realized that someone was trying to help them and that he was Finnish. The officer understood and spoke some Finnish and managed to translate to the rest of the men what Vilho wanted them to do.

After he anointed their eyes, Vilho had them use their kerchiefs to cover their eyes. Using fish line and assorted straps from among the men, he made a life line running from man to the next. He gave them only enough room to move their skis. Then he led them single file toward town.

They barely got started when the Russian officer asked point blank, "Are you Jonas, by any chance?"

Vilho replied hesitantly, "Yes I am."

"How do I know you're not going to lead us over a cliff like you did one of our other patrols?"

"If I was going to kill you, I could have done so at any time. You're as helpless as babies right now. I could have ignored your problem and let you die right here. As for the men that died on that jump, they killed themselves trying to catch and kill me without the skill I have! Tell me, what was I supposed to do?"

After a moment's thought, the officer said quietly, "Our only choice, right now, is to trust you."

"That's right," said Vilho. "I'll lead you close enough to town so someone will find you. Then you can get medical attention for your eyes. We're going to take a circuitous route because I don't want any of you going down steep hills blind."

The officer nodded. "As I said, we have to trust you. Lead on."

It took most of the day to lead the group back to town. There were many problems on the journey with men running into trees and each other because they didn't follow the lead line. Problems occurred in turning corners right. Many times Vilho had to go back down the line to straighten out men and harness. There was a lot of cursing and some crying as the men bumped into each other and trees. They all wondered if they would ever be able to see again. Vilho had to admonish several of them who tried to remove their kerchiefs. They could damage their eyes even more if they didn't keep them covered.

All the time he was leading them, he kept thinking of ways to escape the predicament. He was beginning to regret stopping to help. No matter which way he went he would leave tracks they could follow. If they followed the troop trail, they would find his tracks easily to the trout lake and then follow them all the way back to his cabin, a dilemma to be sure.

The best choice was to stay in the open. He wanted them to follow his current track rather than back track him to his cabin. A big snow storm would hide his trail if he could stay ahead of them that long. If this didn't come about, he wouldn't be able to return to the shelter of his cabin. He could stay away from the patrols for several days and survive with the food and fish he had with him. After the food ran out, it would be tough.

The other hope was, they would back track him to the lake, and be fooled into thinking the cabin was his hideout. There wasn't much hope for the Russians being that stupid, however. The cabin offered little more than shelter for a night. The idea of it, however, might delay them following his tracks long enough for a good snowfall to cover them.

There was no place else to go. If he went into town, they would conduct a house-to-house search for him. In this small town they would find him easily.

It was still daylight when he reached the road leading to the Russian camp. He turned them loose in the middle of the road and told them to stay there. They were on the road to their camp.

"Lieutenant, someone will be along soon," he told them. "Tell them what happened and have them take you the rest of the way to your compound. I can't go any further without the risk of getting caught. You'll be all right. Don't let the men take off their blindfolds until a doctor looks at them. If they do, they risk permanent blindness"

"I understand. Good luck."

"Thanks, I'll need it."

The lieutenant wished he could keep from telling his superiors the name of their benefactor. He knew full well that some of his men knew enough Finnish to know it was Jonas who had helped them. There was no way they could lead them back to the original point, they were blind and blindfolded. It would take some time for trackers to figure out their incoming trail. This would give him time to escape. He felt he owed his life to the man, which indeed he did, and he knew it would be hard to get enthusiastic about hunting him down again.

Vilho formulated a plan for fooling the Russian search but it would involve considerable danger to himself. He eased back into the woods staying on well used trails leading to the small lake used by many for winter fishing.

The snow-blind patrol stood in the road hoping that he told them the truth about where they were. The hard-packed snow beneath their skis told them they were on a road but where and facing what direction had to be trusted. In the distance they heard sleigh bells coming nearer. As the sleigh-bell noise grew louder, the men shouted and waved their arms to get the attention of whoever was coming. Two Russian enlisted men were driving to camp with a load of supplies. They stopped just short of the men, staring at them in disbelief.

"What's the matter with you? Are you all crazy?" asked one of the men on the sleigh.

The lieutenant spoke up. "We're all snow blind. A good samaritan led us this far."

"It was Jonas," one of the men blurted out.

The lieutenant didn't want the word to get out yet, so Jonas would have a little more escape time. He said, "That's who he said he was, but I can hardly believe it."

The teamsters became excited and incredulous. One of the men got down to help the blinded men into the sleigh. As soon as they were loaded the driver whipped up the team, anxious to deliver the news that Jonas was nearby.

On the sleigh, the lieutenant chided the one who had blurted out the news of Jonas. "Here's a man who literally saved your life, and you couldn't wait to turn him in! What kind of man are you?"

"Well, he's our enemy!"

"It didn't appear that way to me with what he did for us," retorted the lieutenant.

The soldier turned his back, knowing the lieutenant was right in what he said but he couldn't bring back his words.

The driver ignored the pleas of the men to get them to a doctor. He wanted the glory of telling headquarters the good news. He slid the sleigh to a stop in front of the command building. Jumping out and running up the steps to the orderly room he shouted, "Jonas is in the area! Jonas is in the area!"

"Of course he is, but just where we would all like to know," said Sergeant Markov sarcastically.

"Really, he's close. He helped this snow-blind patrol! Ask them. They're out in the sleigh."

Markov came out, took one look and began shouting orders. "Get the men to the doctor. We'll question them there. Captain, we have a chance to catch Jonas if we hurry," he shouted back inside. He still wasn't sure if all this was real, but he didn't have any choice but to act.

Gerchenoff said to Markov, "Get Toklat and Chekok. Get a couple of ski patrols mounted right now. When we find out where to look, we'll go after him. Maybe this time we'll get lucky and find that damn renegade."

With his orders given, he took off for the infirmary to question the men.

The patrol arrived when Gerchenoff rushed in, badly out of breath, asking, "What's this about Jonas being in the area?"

The lieutenant replied, "He said he was Jonas when I asked him. I doubt it was him from what I heard about the man. He led us back here after doctoring our eyes for snow blindness.

107

From what I hear this Jonas wouldn't lift one little finger to help a Russian."

"No, it doesn't sound like him," said Gerchenoff, "But we have to act on it anyway. Where were you when all of this happened?"

"We were in the Rock Creek area. Sir, it was my fault we went blind. It was cloudy when we left, and no one bothered to take snow blinders. The sun came out, and before we knew it we were all snow blind. I don't know how long we wandered or in what direction. He found us, doctored our eyes and led us out. We owe our lives to that man!"

"We should be able to backtrack him from the Rock Creek area to his lair," said Gerchenoff ignoring the plea for subtle mercy from the lieutenant.

"I'm sure that he won't be in the area any more. If it really was him, he'll be gone and not return to the area," said the lieutenant.

Gerchenoff went on outlining plans for the hunt. "We'll mount two patrols to that area to see what we can find. First, we'll make a couple of circles to see if we can find the trail where he's going back. Once we find his tracks, we can follow him anywhere. He has to leave tracks in the snow."

"What about the story where his tracks disappeared in an open field?" asked the lieutenant.

Gerchenoff stammered, "I don't know about that. I was there but I still think he tricked us some way."

Rykov, Toklat, and Chekok came into the infirmary. Rykov asked, "What's this rumor about someone seeing Jonas in the area?"

"Well, not really seen, but we think he helped this snow-blind patrol back to base. He told the lieutenant he was Jonas."

"Rubbish, that one wouldn't lift a finger to help any of us, let alone admit he was Jonas," snorted Rykov.

"I don't think we can afford to ignore the information. If it wasn't Jonas, why didn't he stay until help came?"

"No answer to that, sir. We have two patrols ready to go as ordered," said Chekok.

Grudgingly Rykov said, "I suppose you're right. We can't afford to overlook anything that might lead to his capture."

Gerchenoff ordered, "Toklat, you take one patrol and Chekok the other. Jonas, or who ever it was, picked up that patrol in the Rock Creek area. He should have left some tracks. You should be able to find them without much problem. First, cut some big circles to see if we can find out which way he went when he left the patrol. If you don't cut fresh tracks, we'll do a house to house search in town. He has to be in one of the two places. About the only tracks you'll find are the ones going to the fishing lake. Any tracks beyond that area would be worth following. Let's get on with it."

As the men turned to go, Gerchenoff said, "Take a couple of your best trackers. Make sure he hasn't gone right back on the tracks of the patrol he brought in."

With that both men turned on their heels to go to their respective patrols. Neither man was happy to have go on routine patrol. They felt this was a bit beyond them. Anyone else could have handled the patrol.

The two patrols moved to the area where they found the blind patrol on the road. Toklat stopped to take stock of the situation.

He said, "It looks to me like they came up this well-worn trail from the lake. Chekok, you take the left side. I'll take the right side. We'll meet on the other side of the lake. We should cut his trail some where."

Vilho had anticipated the Russians correctly. They were doing just what he thought they would do under the circumstances.

The two patrols came down to the lake and split to go around it. They ignored the fishermen on the lake, one of whom was Vilho. He sat by a fresh-cut hole with his trout from the day before spread out on the ice around him. He looked like one of a dozen other fishermen scattered about the lake.

Vilho crouched low, watching from under the brim of his cap. He saw the patrol split. They went around the lake a scant hundred yards from him. When they were out of sight, he gathered up his gear to follow them. About this time another fisherman came skiing down to go fishing. He saw Vilho gathering up his trout. He stopped to admire his catch.

The fisherman said, "I didn't know there were any trout in this lake."

Vilho replied, "Not many, but there's a spring hole near here and you do catch a few out of there."

"That's good to know, I'll have to try it sometime."

Vilho waited until the fisherman went around a bend in the lake before he picked up his gear to leave.

Vilho thought to himself, *That was kind of rotten, telling him there were trout in the lake. There are none.*

Little did he know the man would fish the area all winter, trying for those trout and not catch a one. He probably wondered what kind of bait Vilho had used to catch that many trout in one place.

Vilho skied up the bank and got on the Toklat patrols tracks. He stayed behind the patrol, using their ski trail. It took him an hour of cautious skiing to catch sight of them. They were going ahead completely unaware that their quarry was on their back trail and watching them. The hunters became the hunted.

The Chekok patrol joined the Toklat patrol when they got to the other side of the lake. Chekok cut the trail of the returning blind patrol on the other side of the lake. His trackers didn't believe he had gone back on his own trail, which indeed, he had not. They followed the blinded patrol tracks until they had to leave them to join up with Toklat.

Vilho watched from the vantage point of a small hillock. He said to himself, "I wish I knew what they were saying down there. It would simplify my decision making."

Toklat said, "I don't know what to do. Clearly, he didn't go back on his own trail or your trackers can't read sign."

110

Chekok bristled, "My trackers are among the best. I would stake my reputation on their ability."

"Oh, don't get all up in the air. I was just joking."

They argued back and forth. Chekok wanted to follow the blind patrol's trail back to Jonas' lair. Toklat was for checking up and down the road to see if he entered the woods elsewhere, but the patrol thought they heard him go in that direction.

The plan was to split up again and each go about three miles parallel to the road, looking for tracks. By then it would be dark, and they would go back to camp after reporting to each other and Gerchenoff. Chekok suspected that the reason Toklat pushed so hard for this tactic was that he didn't want to spend the night out in the woods. Toklat liked his creature comforts. By the time they finished this maneuver it would be time to go back to camp and start anew in the morning.

Vilho watched them split and surmised correctly that they were going to look for entry elsewhere. The longer they delayed following the ski patrol tracks, the greater the chance for a snow storm to cover his tracks.

Gerchenoff ordered the men out the next morning to follow the ski patrol tracks. He also ordered a house-to-house search of the town with the rest of the troops.

Vilho knew Chekok had to have cut the trail where he brought in the snow-blind patrol. He was sure they inspected them closely to see if he had backtracked on that way. Now it would be safe to get on that track. Vilho doubted they would look at the tracks closely again if they did decide to back track him. He followed Chekok's trail until they came to his and the old patrol tracks. Disguising his tracks leaving the Chekok tracks, he got on the patrol tracks to make his way back to the lake cabin.

Clouds were building in the west, but Vilho couldn't be sure when this particular storm would move in, if at all.

It was a bold plan, dependent on a storm coming soon and dropping enough snow. He could avoid the patrols for a few days but then he would be out of food.

He laid out a series of false trails from the cabin. He did as many as he could before dark. That night he cooked more fish for supper and turned into his sleeping bag in the cabin.

Up early the next morning, he laid out more false trails, each doubling back on to itself. They would have to split the patrols into small groups to follow each lead. Each group would have to come back to the cabin to figure which was the real trail and which was not. By then he hoped it would snow and they would lose his track.

"At worst I'll have to spend another day away from the cabin. Surely, it'll snow in the next two days the way those clouds look."

It didn't snow the next day so Vilho played fox and hounds once more. He laid out a series of false trails leading them farther and farther from the original track. The patrol arrived and obligingly followed the freshest track.

In the middle of the next day, it started to snow a few large flakes. Toklat looked at the sky and knew they had a big storm coming. He didn't want to stay out in a blizzard. The snow would soon cover all tracks and before they couldn't untangle all the false leads.

Toklat and Chekok discussed the problems. They both decided it was time to go back before they got caught in a big storm and couldn't get back.

"What I don't understand," said Toklat, "is how he got here without leaving tracks. One of those false trails must be the real one leading from town to here."

Chekok agreed saying, "I think that's right but where does he stay? It can't be in this rustic cabin, although it looks like he has been using this place off and on."

"I think Gerchenoff was right when he said that he didn't stay anywhere for long," said Toklat.

Chekok said, "We'll have a starting place when this storm lets up. I would think his real base might not be all that far from here. After the storm, we should send up a fresh patrol and search the area."

Toklat gave the order for the two patrols to move out and head back to town. The patrol rejoiced. They didn't like following this will'o-the-wisp, ghost, or whatever. No one wanted to spend another night on the trail. They would have to hurry if they hoped to get home before dark and the snow storm hit in earnest.

Vilho watched from a far hilltop as the patrols reversed their direction. He watched to make sure that they were really going back. Turning his skis toward his own cabin, he knew he had out-foxed them again.

Chapter Nine

Resistance Movement

NEED WAS BUILDING FOR THE RESISTANCE MOVEMENT. It was growing fast and needed extra supplies to keep going.

Reluctantly, Vilho left Mary alone while he went to Kiivijarvi to deal with the problems facing the freedom movement. He worried about Mary, but she was a strong woman and was coming around from the rape and was feeling like her old self again.

His usual first stop was the Lehtinen house. From there Matt accompanied him to the Boar's Head bringing him up to date on the latest news.

Mika gave him his usual booming welcome as he let him into the back door of the store room.

Mika said, "We need to get right down to business. The town of Koskela is coming into its own in the resistance. Arne Sivula and Jacob Korpi were transferred there as training cadres for the small outpost. I know you know them as they were in your group. They've organized a new group, but they need weapons, ammunition, and money to keep going."

"Most of the rifles from the raid are still stored. I think it would be safe to let them have some. We'd have to be careful to let them know where they came from. If some of the rifles fell into Russian hands, they would suddenly be in a lot of trouble," Vilho responded.

"They requested twenty rifles and ammunition. I don't see any problem with that, but how are we going to get the weapons to them?"

"Who is usually on the supply-wagon run to Koskela? If it's Finn drivers and not Russians, they might at least be sympathetic to our cause."

"I see what you mean. We might be able to smuggle them on one of the supply wagons if the drivers are with us."

"Have you any way of finding out who the drivers are and when they leave?" asked Vilho.

"I think so," said Mika. "How long can you stay this time? Is Mary feeling better? Does she mind staying alone for the time you're with us?"

"I can stay a few more days, and, yes, Mary is doing better. She says she doesn't mind staying alone. I think she really does, but she'd never say so. In any case, this work is important. I won't shirk from the resistance. She is as much for freedom as any of us."

"I'll try to find out something tonight. In the meantime, slip upstairs and relax. If I find out anything, I'll come up. I'll fix you something to eat and bring it up later."

Vilho relaxed in one of Mika's easy chairs and was soon fast asleep. He woke with start as he heard Mika's key in the lock.

As Mika came in, Vilho said, "I must feel safe here. This is the second time I've fallen asleep in your chair."

"That's good. I've never had anyone want to come up or search the place. I'm sure the Russians have no idea I'm involved in the freedom movement."

"Have you found out anything about the supply wagons?"

"They leave day after tomorrow and both drivers are with our unit. The only possible hitch might be that a Russian officer goes with them. This happens seldom as most of them like to ride their own horses rather than the slow freight wagons."

"We'll have to take that chance and be ready to load the rifles on the wagons. They have to pass right by the intersection of the Rock Quarry road where the guns are hidden. A light buggy would suffice to move the guns from their hiding place to the wagons. If everything goes well on that score, I can go cross country and beat the wagons to Koskela. We can have men waiting to unload the guns and ammunition before they get to town."

"Your contact in Koskela is a restaurant-tavern owner by the name of Waino Keski who I recruited into the group. His place is called Ilta Tallo, and it's on the southern outskirts of town, right on the road. He can get word to the people to move the guns. You'll have to hurry to beat the wagons and get everything set up, though. When we know the guns are going to be on the wagons, you can leave."

Everything went as planned, and, as it turned out, no Russians would be on the supply wagons. One of the group of resistance people hurried on ahead to get the buggy moving with the guns. It took only a few minutes to off load the guns to one of the supply wagons.

Vilho said to the drivers. "We'll meet you somewhere south of town to off load the guns. I'll make sure our meeting place is at least a mile from town. If you don't see us by the time you're within a half mile of town, unload the guns and hide them in the woods. If no one contacts you before you have to leave, contact Waino Keski, owner of the Ilta Tallo tavern."

He took off at a brisk trot into the forest. He knew he could save hours by going as the crow flies plus he could travel faster than the lumbering supply wagons. Still, there was an urgency in his stride to get to Koskela with plenty of time to arrange for unloading and hiding the guns. Distribution would have to be made by leaders of the local resistance group.

It was an enjoyable walk through the forest for Vilho. He always liked the solitude and serenity. It was as a balm to his soul to glory in nature.

He arrived in Koskela near dark, knowing it would be the next day before the wagons got there. The tavern was his first stop.

Once inside, he looked around for Waino. He spotted him from Mika's description and gave him the sign of the resistance which was a rapidly opening and closing of the fist. Waino saw the sign and nodded. Vilho relaxed and ordered a glass of wine from the man behind the bar.

Waino sat down alongside Vilho saying. "Didn't I meet you a couple of months ago in Kiivijarvi at Mika's place?"

Vilho going along said. "Yes, I think we did meet. I was down this way and thought to drop in and say hello."

"I'm glad you did. How is Mika anyway?"

"He's just fine. I was with him not long ago."

As the bartender moved on down the bar, Waino said, "My bartender is Finn, but he's new and I'm not sure about his convictions. For now let's talk business only while he's out of earshot."

Vilho leaned in close. "We have twenty of the new Winchester rifles from an earlier raid. We took them off the Russian army. They're coming in with the regular shipment of supplies from Kiivijarvi. We need to unload them south of town."

The man nodded. "We can do that. How did you manage to get the Russians to haul our guns?"

"The wagon drivers are Finns and members of our group in Kiivijarvi. We loaded them after they left the post."

"It's nice of the Russkies to help us in our cause this way."

"I thought so too."

The bartender came their way, so they switched their talk to news in Kiivijarvi and Mika.

The bartender left, and Waino said. "When do you expect the wagons to arrive here?"

"Sometime late tomorrow afternoon."

"No problem. I can have as many men as you need."

"Ten should be enough unless we can get a buggy or wagon south of town to haul them."

"A buggy is no problem. I have a rig that'll do fine. I go fishing south of town quite often so it won't look at all suspicious."

"All we'll need is you and me and the buggy. The drivers of the wagons can help us load the guns into your rig. The fewer people knowing about this the better. I need you to let the people know where the guns came from. If they get caught with them, there could be lots of trouble for your people here and for us in Kiivijarvi."

"Understood. I thought we might get Arne and Jacob to help. They're the leaders of the group and might have some idea where we can hide the guns and ammunition until we can get them distributed."

"Good idea. I'd like to talk to them about coordinating our efforts to oust the Russians."

"They'll be in some time this evening. I'll let them know. You could meet with them here in the tavern. No one knows you here, so it wouldn't look suspicious. We don't have that many Russians coming in here anyway. This is nothing like the contingent at Kiivijarvi."

The next afternoon, Arne and Jacob came to the tavern, and the four of them left with fishing rods showing.

"We have an early start, so we might as well actually fish a little to really make it look legitimate," said Waino.

"You can't fool us, Waino," said Arne. "We know you would rather fish than do most anything."

Jacob and Arne contrasted in every way. Jacob was tall, raw-boned, blue eyed with a ruddy complexion. Arne was short, squat with a smooth, white complexion. Jacob was quiet while Arne was talking all the time. Arne used gestures heavily to emphasize a point. Two things they had in common was blond hair and a fierce love of freedom.

Waino pulled the buggy off the road near a small stream. It didn't take long to catch a sizable mess of trout.

Arne commented, "We got our supper for tonight if we can get Waino to cook them."

118

"No problem," replied Waino. "I would like a nice meal of fish myself. Come by about six or seven, and we'll all eat."

It wasn't long before they heard the distant rumble and creaking of the heavy wagons. Shortly, they came around the bend in the road.

Vilho said, "Don't do anything until I make sure we have the same drivers on board that left Kiivijarvi."

Vilho walked up to meet the wagons, and then gave the all-clear to the rest of the group.

The guns and ammunition were quickly unloaded into the buggy, and the freight wagons continued on their way.

Arne and Jacob directed them to an old house on the edge of town where they hid the guns under the floor.

Jacob said, "No need to worry. The house is owned by an old man sympathetic to our cause. We have used it before as a hiding place, so he won't do anything without checking with us first."

Arne said. "We have to get back to the barracks for a short while to check on our recruits. We left them on a training session while we came with you. We'll see you tonight for the fish dinner."

That evening, the whole group settled in on a big table for the fish. Waino did a superb job of preparing everything. The fish were done to perfection, and everyone ate their fill.

Everyone sat back and relaxed, full and content, having a small glass of brandy to top everything off, when Vilho noticed a lone Russian move up to the bar and take a hard look at Vilho.

Vilho said quietly, "Don't look now, but we have been discovered. That Russian at the bar was in Kiivijarvi when I was there. I am sure he recognized me. I don't worry about myself as I'm already a fugitive, but they'll connect me with you and then you with the resistance movement. I'm going to have to kill him."

Jacob asked, "Are you sure?"

"What do you mean, am I sure? I'm sure he recognized me and yes, he'll have to be killed."

The Russian picked up his glass, walked over to their table pulling up a chair as he came.

He said in perfect Finnish, "I know who you are Vilho, and that this must be part of the resistance movement."

Everyone sat dumbfounded for the moment with the revelation that this Russian knew and was speaking perfect Finnish.

"I sat there at the bar contemplating all of this for a while. I knew you would have to kill me to keep this quiet. All this went through my mind quickly. Many things jelled just now that I forced myself not to think about in the past. I wondered to myself why I learned to speak your language. I felt uneasy about the way we treated you people. It came to me now that I want to become a part of your group."

"Do you really want to become a part of our group or is this the best way you could think of to save your life?" asked Vilho.

"I realize how ridiculous this all sounds but hear me out. Find another of your men away from here, have him look through the window so he can identify me. If something happens to any of you because of me he will kill me."

Sounds all right to me," said Jacob, "We can use someone on the inside to feed us information."

"I'm willing to do that for your cause," said the Russian, "but if they catch me, I want you to make some effort to get me out. I would want to be transferred to another unit and become one of you."

"Fair enough," said Arne.

Vilho said nothing. He was not one to trust the motives of any Russian under any circumstances. Grudgingly he admitted to himself that this one might be different.

"My name is Yuri Yanov but everyone calls me YY because of my initials and because I ask so many questions."

Yuri was of medium height and build with black hair and dark eyes set in deep sockets giving him a ghost-like look. This was counteracted by his impish smile. His nose was thin and blade-like giving him the look of a bird of prey.

Yuri finished his drink and said, "I have to get back, but I will come here again and see what kind of information you need. I'll get it if it's at all possible."

When Yuri cleared the door, Arne said, "I think he's going to be one of us, but there's no point in taking chances. I think we ought to disperse. If any one of us is picked up, the rest should go into the wilderness. I am glad Waino wasn't at our table, at least he'll be spared if Yuri turns out to be a traitor."

Jacob said, "I think he's sincere, but I too feel we should not be very trusting until he proves himself to us."

"I don't trust him at all," said Vilho, "but then I've never trusted any Russian. You're the ones who are going to work with him. I'm going to head back to Kiivijarvi and my Mary. If something bad does happen, have Waino send word to Kiivijarvi."

Vilho left for home with some misgivings about the Russian joining their ranks, but he felt it was a problem for the ones at Koskela.

Vilho carefully made his way back to his hidden cabin in the forest. After joyous reunion, Mary burst out, "I'm sure I'm in a family way. My time of the month is two weeks overdue. All ready I feel different. I know that sounds crazy."

Vilho gave her a big hug and kiss saying, "I'm glad for the both of us. I really want this. We'll have to think about it when your time comes and how we can handle it.

"I would like to have the baby here if possible. Do you think you could handle it?"

Vilho considered. "I don't think so, I've done a lot of things but . . . this one might be more than I can handle."

"We have some time to think about it."

"Maybe we could get Anna Lehtinen to come here. I know she's helped in some births in the past."

"I would like her to be the one if we do have some one here but would she come for that long?"

"I don't know. I'll ask her the next time I go into town."

"Do you think it possible for me to go into town with you the next time you go? I'm so lonesome to see some other faces and talk to some other people?"

"That's understandable. I think we could take the chance. You could stay at the Lehtinen's. Not many people at the post know about our relationship. Chances are the people that know wouldn't be involved in a search of their place. They would be looking for Jonas. They might not make a search while you were there."

"It's settled then."

Chapter Ten

A Son Is Born

As Vilho promised, he took Mary with him on his next visit to town. Anna was delighted to see them both and more delighted when she heard they were going to have a baby.

Vilho tried to get away, but Anna insisted he have coffee and fresh-baked cinnamon rolls. The rolls were good but Vilho was impatient to find out from Mika how things were going.

It was not quite dark when he and Matt arrived at the Boar's Head. Matt went inside to get Mika to open the store room door.

Mika came quickly to let Vilho in. As soon as he was inside Mika said, "You crazy egotistical fool, why did you have to sign your name to the murder of Yuri Tokarev? They might still be trying to figure out what happened. Now they know it was you."

"I wanted to show them they can't get away with treating us like that without suffering the consequences."

"I know all that, but now they're going to hunt you down just as hard as they've been hunting Jonas."

"They have to catch me first."

"The other dumb thing you did was to say it was your woman. You didn't give her name, but I'm sure they'll figure that one out. That not only makes Mary a fugitive, but puts her family at risk as well."

Vilho hadn't considered that. "I guess it wasn't too bright of me to get Mary into the fray that way. She's at the Lehtinen's right now. She was lonesome so I let her come with me."

"Vilho, I think you'd better get her and head back to the wilderness as soon as possible. If the Russians happen to check the Lehtinens again and find her, there'll be hell to pay."

"I didn't get time to tell you that she's pregnant. That's one of the reasons we came in, to see if Anna would come to the cabin when she's due."

"She's pregnant? All the more reason to get her out of here. She isn't pregnant from Yuri is she?"

"No, it's my doing for sure. I think Mary might have killed herself and the baby if it was Yuri's."

"I'm serious Vilho, I think you ought to get away as soon as possible."

"You're probably right, but I need to update you on the happenings in Koskela."

"Can't it wait?"

"It could, but I'm here now so I might as well fill you in and then leave. Mary will be disappointed with the short stay."

They talked for an hour with Mika getting more nervous all the time. He worried more about Mary being caught at the Lehtinen house. He knew Vilho could take care of himself.

They said goodbye, and Mika went back into the restaurant to let Matt know Vilho was ready to leave.

They met out in front and walked in the shadows to the Lehtinen house.

As they neared the house Matt said, "Something's wrong. The warning shade is all the way down. We better find out what's going on before we go barging in."

Matt eased up to a kitchen window to have a peek. He ducked back down immediately and said in a whisper, "They have Mary, Anna, and my father tied up. They have coats draped over their shoulders. I think they're leaving soon."

"How many are there?"

"I saw only two, but there might be some more in the other room."

"Let's go back out to the road," whispered Vilho urgently.

Back on the road, Vilho said, "Take my rifle. I have my pistol. We'll wait and see if they come out. There's only one road they can take. We can go ahead and ambush them. I know just the spot."

A few minutes later, two soldiers came out of the house herding Anna, Toivo, and Mary ahead of them.

Vilho said, "There's only two of them. You back me up with the rifle. I can get close without them seeing I have a pistol. Let's get on up the road."

They stopped at a small bushy spot by the side of the road to wait. Vilho said, "I'll act like I'm heading toward town. When I get abreast of them I'll shoot them both. If something happens and I don't get them both, back me up with the rifle."

"Why not let me get one and you the other?"

"That rifle is too obvious. I need to get close so we don't endanger our people."

As the group approached, Vilho stepped out of the shadows as though he just relieved himself. The Russians were several feet behind their captors and not worried. Neither one knew what happened when Vilho made the two quick shots. Mary muffled a short scream when she realized who did the shooting.

Matt came up shortly with his rifle at the ready but there was no need.

Vilho said quickly, "Matt help me turn the men around so it looks like they were heading toward your house."

They struggled for a few minutes to get the men turned around without making it look obvious.

Vilho said, "Strip off their ammunition belts and rifles to make it look like they were killed for them. I'll take those with me. It wouldn't do for you to get caught with them. All of you go back home. I'll take Mary and head for the cabin. If the

Russians question you, tell them you never saw anyone. Hopefully, they'll think the men were killed on the way to your house. If they expected to pick up anyone, they would have sent a bigger group. This had to be a routine check on your place."

Toivo said, "The two Russians thought Mary was Jonas' Emma and that they had a real prize. They assumed that Mary was her. That was the reason they were taking us back to headquarters."

"I was wondering how they connected her to me. Now I know there was no connection."

Vilho and Mary headed down the road to pick up the trail to the cabin while the Lehtinen's returned home.

"Oh, Vilho, I was so scared. I was sure you would walk in on them and be captured or do something foolish and be killed. I wasn't afraid for myself."

"It's over and hopefully they won't connect the killings to us or the Lehtinens."

The next morning found Vilho and Mary safely back in their wilderness cabin. About the same time, the two bodies were discovered by a man on a delivery wagon headed for the post.

Captain Gerchenoff and Major Rykov met at the scene along with other officers and enlisted men from the post.

Rykov asked, "Has anything been touched? Where are their rifles and ammo belts? What were they doing here so late at night?"

Gerchenoff calmly answered, "No, nothing has been touched, this is how they were found. It appears they were murdered for their rifles and ammo probably by some of the Jonas group or possibly Jonas himself although there's no Jonas Ghost emblem around. The men were going on a routine check of the Lehtinen premises in case Jonas or Vilho happened to be there. We have been making surprise visits from time to time."

Rykov asked, "Do you suppose they found Jonas, Vilho, or both there and were taking them in and some of their companions killed our men and rescued them?"

"It's possible, I suppose, but the way the bodies are laying and everything I would tend to think they were headed toward their house and not away from it."

Rykov was arrogant, haughty and had no feeling for men in his command other than what they could do to help him rise in the ranks. He ruled with an iron fist.

Time passed and Mary was getting closer to the baby's delivery date.

Vilho said, "I better get Anna to come out to take care of you when the baby comes. Will you be all right by yourself for a couple of days?"

"Of course, the baby isn't any where close to due. I can still get around and do things fine. I know it's a little early but if we wait too long, the baby might come when you're gone. I don't think I could deliver it by myself."

Vilho's trip into town was uneventful. He arrived at the hilltop overlooking the Lehtinen house before dark and had to wait before crossing the open ground.

Anna was the only one home, and she greeted him warmly saying, "The men are at a resistance meeting but will be back before too long. They said it would only be a couple of hours and it's nearly that now."

"I came in to see if I might get you to come to our cabin to help in the birth of our child?"

"Of course, I'll come," smiled the motherly woman. "You might ask Toivo if he would like to come as well. We talked about it, and he wanted to do a little fishing with you. Do you think it would be too crowded?

"It'll be a bit crowded, but we can manage. It's summer. If it gets too crowded Toi and I could sleep outdoors."

Shortly, Toivo and Matt came from the meeting. They were both glad to see Vilho and both started talking at once.

Matt said, "I'll shut up and let father talk."

"Thank you Matt, I knew I taught you to respect your elders."

"It's not that so much. I just know you'll wind up telling it your way no matter what I say."

Turning to Vilho, Toivo said, "We have a good group right now, and it's growing. Our people are coming around to realizing that their destiny is in their own hands. From now on all we need is good leadership and guidance, that's where you come in. Our people look to men like you to lead them out of this yoke of bondage. It's getting easier all the time to lead them."

"I'm not sure about me being a leader. I have enough trouble taking care of myself and Mary and now a little one on the way. I just don't know."

"We have to have men like you whom the others respect. They'll follow you blindly."

"I still don't know. We'll talk about it later. Right now I came to get Anna to help with the birth of our child. If you would like to come, we could get in a little fishing while the women talk."

Toivo's eyes lit up. He said, "I was hoping you'd ask me. I'm looking forward to all the good fishing spots you've located."

"I know a few. We can catch enough for a meal or two."

Anna said, "Get your things together, Toivo, and we'll get on our way. I can be packed in five minutes and then help you locate everything you can't find. Vilho, can you find your way by starlight? I think we ought to be on our way this very minute. The Russians have been here so often I am beginning to think our house is part of the post."

"Yes, I can find our way. There's going to be a good moon tonight so that'll help. We'll get there in plenty of time for breakfast."

Anna said, "Matt, if the Russians ask, tell them we went to visit my sister in Koskela for a while as she's very sick and needs some extra care. We will be back right after the baby is born. You take care of yourself."

It turned out to be a beautiful moonlit night. The woods were soft and pleasant with a slight breeze stirring. The sun was peeking up over the tree tops when they reached the cabin.

Vilho helped Toivo and Anna around the alarms he had to let him know if the Russians came near. The old hawk screamed as they came close to its nest. Vilho didn't give the customary greeting bird call as Mary was already half way across the clearing to meet them.

Everyone exchanged hugs and kisses. Mary said, "Come on in and let me put on a pot of coffee and start breakfast."

Anna looked around in awe saying, "I can't believe Jonas built all of this for Emma and they lived here. I visualized a small, rustic cabin. I felt sorry for Emma having to live like a poor peasant. This is really nice."

Mary said, "You haven't seen the inside yet. There's a lot more than meets the casual eye."

They all went inside. Mary put on a pot of coffee before she took them on a tour of all the nice things Jonas had built into the place for Emma.

"Tomorrow, Toivo, I'll take you fishing," said Vilho. "I can show you where the fish are, but it'll be up to you to catch them. If we don't catch a nice mess, we go without supper. Today we'll fix a nice bed for you and Anna in the sauna. It'll give you some privacy. We'll have to take out the pallet when we want to take a sauna, but that shouldn't be too hard. Right now I'll heat up the sauna. There are rain clouds forming fast, so I know the Russians won't be sending out any patrols this day and see our smoke."

After breakfast, they all had a sauna and sat around catching up on the latest news in town and talking about the coming baby.

Anna asked, "Have you picked out a name for the baby yet?"

Mary said, "No, we haven't. I'm a bit superstitious about a name until after it's born."

"Probably just as well," replied Anna, "Sometimes you pick a boy or girl's name and then it turns out to be the opposite. Best thing is to hope for a healthy, normal child."

Vilho and Toivo enjoyed each other's company and did a lot of fishing while they were waiting. The weather stayed fair. A few days they couldn't have a daytime fire because the Russians might be on patrol in the area. Days like that they stayed close to the cabin and had a cold lunch. By night they lit fires so the women could cook hot meals.

One morning after a bad storm, Mary woke up and told Vilho she wasn't feeling well.

"Maybe the baby is on the way," said Vilho.

"I don't think so. I just feel odd that's all. No contractions or anything like that."

"You'd better talk to Anna. She will know what's going on."

"I'll wait until they get up. I don't want her to think I worry about every little thing. I'll get started on breakfast."

Ann came out of their sauna shortly saying, "Mary, I would have cooked breakfast. You should be taking life easy."

"I didn't feel well, so I got up and wanted to do something useful."

"You're not feeling well? What are you feeling?"

"I feel odd is all. Kind of far away or something."

"I would venture to guess that the baby will be here in a day or two at the most."

"I hope so. I feel like a big awkward cow with my belly sticking out so far."

Toivo came out a little later and asked Vilho, "How about trying those small spring holes down on Rock Creek again? We had some good fishing down there."

"Sounds good. We better dig for a few worms around the edge of the garden. Last time we had to turn over a lot of rocks by the stream to find enough."

Toivo and Vilho were at the spring holes, and both were catching fish, when Vilho said quietly, "Put your pole down and follow me quickly."

Toivo gave him a puzzled look.

Vilho said in a hoarse whisper, "Now, Toivo, now!"

Toivo dropped his pole and started after Vilho.

Vilho had to help him scramble over rocks and through brush to a small depression behind some boulders. They could see the stream and the trail beyond.

Toivo, gasping for breath, asked, "What's wrong?"

"Be quiet. Some Russians are coming!"

Shortly a crow flapped by, giving an alarm call, a clear signal that someone was coming.

Out of the corner of his eye Vilho saw movement up the trail. He whispered to Toivo, "Here they come, whatever you do, don't move as they go by. Don't move or say anything until I tell you."

Toivo's eyes flew wide open in amazement as he watched the horse patrol move down the trail.

Vilho sat stock still. Toivo followed suite.

A few minutes later, a lone rider came down the trail not making a single sound. He stopped every few minutes to look around. He stopped opposite Vilho and Toivo and stared for a few minutes before riding on.

Vilho let out a breath and whispered, "We can go in a few minutes as soon as he gets well out of sight."

They crawled out of their hiding place, picked up their fish and headed for the cabin.

Toivo was visibly shaken by the ordeal. He asked Vilho, "How did you know they were coming? I didn't see òr hear a thing. How did you know there was another rider coming?"

"First of all, you get a feeling in the forest when something different is going on. It's a subtle change you get to recognize. The following rider I knew about from Jonas telling me, and I have seen them myself since."

"How come that following rider made no noise compared to the first group? I thought for sure he saw us when he stopped and looked our way for so long."

They use no saddles or bridles or anything that will make noise. They have leather boots on the horses hooves with ridges sewn in them for traction. They do go through the forest like ghosts. They think someone will see the main patrol go by and come out in the open to be seen by the following rider. If we had moved, he would have spotted us. He probably saw something that didn't look right, but when we didn't move he went on."

Back at the cabin Anna met them at the door.

Toivo blurted out, "We had an adventure! We were nearly caught by a Russian patrol!"

"We had an adventure here, too. Vilho, you have a fine healthy son, and Mary is doing fine."

Vilho hugged Anna and said, "I would shout for joy, but I don't know just where those pesky Russians are right now."

"Go in and see Mary and your son."

Mary was lying still, almost asleep when Vilho came in. She smiled and pulled the covers back to show him their sleeping son nestled against her body.

"He looks so little and wrinkled," said Vilho dismayed.

"Anna said most babies look like that when they're first born. Anna assured me he is perfect in every way."

"I'm glad it's over, and I'm glad you're doing fine."

"Anna said she would stay as long as it takes to get me to the point where I can take care of him myself. What would you like to name your son?"

"I thought of a lot of names. I thought for sure it would be girl, and you would want to name her. I had a friend when I was young called Marti. They moved away, and I missed him very much. I kind of like that name but you have a say in it too."

"I like the sound of it myself. Let's make his second name Jonas for your other friend."

"I like that too. I thought of that for his first name but with the price on Jonas' head and all I thought we ought to name him something else."

Toivo and Anna came in. Toivo had to see and admire the new baby.

They related the incident of the Russian patrol.

Vilho said, "We'll have to watch our fire smoke until we're sure they're out of the area. I hope Marti will see freedom in his life time."

Chapter Eleven

Gold

MARTI WAS GROWING UP FAST. He had learned to crawl and was taking his first toddling steps. He had curly blond hair and blue eyes and a sunny disposition. He was into everything. They had to watch him every minute, he was so active. Vilho found it harder and harder to leave them to take care of resistance business.

A trip to Koskela to help formulate plans to harass the Russians brought him face to face with Yuri Yanov again.

His first stop in Koskela was with Waino at the Ilta Tallo Tavern. Waino recognized him immediately and sat down to talk.

"Everything is going fine so far. We have distributed guns and ammunition to everyone who's active. We didn't have enough for the whole group, but it will do for now."

Vilho said, "Mika heard about a Russian payroll shipment headed for this post and some other ones north of here. The shipment is in gold coin. It's too far for our Kiivijarvi group to try to intercept, but your group could do it, preferably before they distributed any of the gold to the Russians stationed here."

"I think we can handle it. Do you know for sure it's coming and when?"

"Don't know any of the details. Maybe it's only a rumor, but they have been paying off in gold once in a while. Do you think our friend Yuri could get some details?"

"He may be able to help. He has given us quite a bit of reliable information already. I believe he's sincere in wanting to help our freedom movement."

"I'll take your word for it, but you know I don't trust any Russian."

"I still have reservations myself, but I'm coming around to believing he's genuine."

"If Yuri gave us information on this shipment, it would go a long way towards convincing me that he really is on our side."

"He's been coming in here almost every night. I expect he'll be in later. We can ask him if he's heard anything or if he can find out anything."

Arne and Jacob, the two main leaders of the movement in the Koskela area came into the tavern. They immediately recognized Vilho and sat down to talk. Vilho told them about the possible shipment of gold coin coming into the area.

Arne said, "We can accomplish a lot more with gold. Their scrip money makes it difficult to buy supplies, such as guns. Gold makes for a better negotiating position on the price of anything we need."

Jacob said, "Maybe it's a trap to try to get us to go for the gold. This is the first time I ever heard of the Russians paying off in gold."

"I've heard of it a few times," said Waino.

Yuri Yanov came in, and they waved him over to their table.

Yuri shook hands all around and said, "Vilho, it's good to see you again. I hope they told you about the information I've been feeding them."

Jacob asked point blank, "Do you know anything about a shipment of gold coin coming here for payroll and then going north to pay some other stations?"

"No, but there's been some rumors floating they plan to do it because of the government scrip becoming subject to devaluation or more inflation. People are thinking if the Russians leave, the scrip will be useless. Most people try to get away from accepting it for payment. I'll try to find out what's going on tomorrow."

The next night Yuri came in very excited. His excitement was contagious. Before he could say anything, they assumed that the gold rumor was true.

"You're right, they're shipping some gold coin in, but there's a catch to it all. They're going to set a trap for the resistance movement with it at the same time."

"What kind of trap?" said Vilho. "I'd love to take the gold out from under their noses without springing the trap."

"They'll spread the word about the gold coming but plan to follow behind the wagons with a troop of cavalry. The cavalry will be far enough behind so they won't be seen but within a short running distance. A signal man following closely behind the wagons but in the woods will fire his rifle in the event of attack. The troop will come on the run to grab any would-be robbers."

"That doesn't give us much time to do the job," said Jacob.

"I don't want to take the chance of losing some of our men. The gold is tempting but is it going to be worth the risk?" asked Arne.

Vilho said, "Maybe we can figure a way to get it without risk."

"How?" asked Jacob.

"If we can keep the signal man from firing his rifle, we might have enough time to grab the wagon. If the troops don't hear a signal they'll keep their distance. We take over and run like crazy. We dump the gold in a good hiding place and be gone before they know what happened."

"It sounds good, but there are a lot of ifs connected with the operation," said Arne.

"Let's look at the route coming to town for several miles back and see if there's anyplace we might ambush the wagon."

135

"We'll have to make sure we neutralize the signal man, but we won't even know which side of the road he'll be following," said Jacob.

"We can have two or more men on each side of the road if we do decide to try for the gold," said Vilho.

Arne said, "It'll have to be up to you and Waino to check out the road. Jake and I have to train new recruits tomorrow, and I'm sure Yuri will have to work."

"No problem," said Waino, "I can say we're going on a fishing trip again."

The group broke up early, leaving Waino and Vilho sitting at the table by themselves.

"If Yuri is going to set a trap for us, this would be an excellent opportunity," said Vilho.

"I thought the same thing," said Waino. "We must take precautions in case it's a double trap."

The next morning Waino and Vilho were off in Waino's buggy to check out the route the gold wagon would follow. South of town, they found where the road made two turns with almost a mile between.

Vilho said, "This looks like a good spot. We could catch the signal man along here somewhere on this straight stretch. When the wagon turns the first corner we grab it and run. The troops would think the wagon was around that corner and then the next. They would ride blissfully on as long as they heard no signal. They wouldn't be aware we stole the wagon until they got into town and it wasn't there."

"Sounds good but what do we do with the drivers on the wagon? How do we keep the troops from following wagon tracks wherever we take it?"

"Two good questions. We blindfold and tie up the drivers. Then, we never take the wagon itself, just the contents. Chances are the gold is in bags but even if it isn't we can have horses with saddlebags to transfer the gold. Our tracks will be wiped out by the troop coming through. The horses towing the wagon will go on by themselves."

"It might work," conceded Waino, "We have to hide the horses and riders far enough in the woods where the wagon drivers can't see them until we know the signal man is out. How do we do that?"

"First, let's find a place to hide our troops. We can have one man hidden near the road to pick up a signal from those ambushing their signal man. After the wagon passes, he runs to our hidden troops, and we go for the gold."

Some scouting revealed a small gully that would hide men and horses from the road. It was a short run from there to the road to intercept the gold wagon.

Backtracking down the road, they found spots for the ambushers to hide on both sides of the road.

"This is about all we can do for now," said Vilho. "We need to get back to town and get everyone organized so it goes off without a hitch."

Later that night they met by ones and twos at the Ilta Tallo. Each man stopped by Vilho's table to get his specific assignment and left shortly afterwards, so a large gathering wouldn't be observed by the Russians.

"Now, all we need is some specifics on the arrival of the gold shipment," said Vilho.

Waino replied, "Yuri will probably come by tonight. I hope he'll have the information we need."

Yuri came in, eyes shining with excitement, the words tumbled out in a torrent, "The shipment is on its way and will arrive here on Thursday afternoon next week. They plan to drop off some gold here and leave the next day with the rest."

"Let's hope we can save them that hard and arduous trip north by relieving them of all that gold here," quipped Vilho.

They all laughed, and Waino said, "Yes, I'd hate to see them have to make such a hard trip."

Thursday morning found everyone assembled on the road into Koskela. Vilho and Waino sent everyone to their specific tasks. Though the gold wagon was not expected for some time, it was important that everyone be in position early.

Time dragged, and the men fidgeted, waiting for the action. All of the men, with the exception of Vilho, were new to this kind of action and were nervous. They told jokes and talked excessively to hide their fear and apprehension. Each man wondered if he would perform well in front of his friends.

By mid-afternoon tensions hummed. The wagon could come by any time. Men had been stationed in advance of the troops to let the hidden riders know when the wagon approached and when the Russian signal men had been eliminated. Everyone waited tensely for news.

The first man nearly caused a stampede among the hidden horses as he burst into the gully with the news that the gold wagon had been spotted. This reaction gave Vilho considerable concern. These men would give themselves away before they could accomplish their goal if he he didn't settle them down.

"All men off your horses," he ordered. "Hold their noses so they won't whinny and give away our position when the wagon comes by. We have to wait until their signal men are out of action. Not a sound."

For what seemed like hours, the resisters waited. Then the gold wagon slowly rumbled by. Everyone knew that the Russian point men would be close behind it. This was the moment of truth for them. Either they would soon implement the rest of their plan or they would be running full out with the Russian horsemen on their heels.

The runner came again, this time making his final approach into the gully with more caution. He announced that their ambushers had indeed neutralized the Russian signal men.

"Mount up," ordered Vilho. "We go to the gold wagon as fast as possible the minute it turns the corner."

The wagon drivers were surprised as the troops rode out of the woods directly behind them. Two men with hoods climbed into the wagon tied and blindfolded the drivers. Vilho spat orders in Russian, and several men he had coached answered back. They used hand signals to keep the operation going smoothly and silently. Vilho continued giving orders in

Russian as they took bags of gold coins and loaded them directly into saddlebags. Some bags had to be tied and slung across the saddles as the saddlebags weren't adequate to hold it all. The transfer proceeded quickly as riders filed by and left, loaded with gold. When all of it had been taken away, the drivers were left with their empty wagon, bound and gagged so they could only helplessly be carried wherever the horses wished. The heavy draft horses, however, had one pace only; they plodded placidly onward, following the road, as though nothing happened, though they may have appreciated that their load had been considerably lightened by the Finns. The horses followed the road right into town and headed straight along the main road, not knowing or caring that they had been intended to turn onto the post road. They were out of sight by the time the following cavalry troops rode into town, turned onto the post road and headed for the post.

When they arrived in the compound and dismounted, the post commander came out and asked, "Where's the gold wagon?"

The troop commander gave him a look of confused incredulity. "You mean it's not here?"

"It never arrived. How the hell did you mange to lose it?"

The troop commander ordered his men to remount their horses. "Sir, we followed it the whole way. We even had signal men on point in the woods. No signal was ever given. We'll backtrack and find it, sir."

"You better find it!" shot back the post commander, "or there will be hell to pay all the way back to St. Petersburg."

The cavalry troop at full gallop saw where the wagon had proceeded straight into town, and the troop commander gave a premature sigh of relief to think that the drivers simply had taken a wrong turn. The mounted troops thundered through the town after the wagon. They caught up with the plodding horses on the other side of town and quickly brought the team and wagon to a halt. Then they discovered the drivers still tied and gagged in the bed of the wagon.

As soon as the drivers were freed, they were flooded with a torrent of questions. "Where's the gold? What happened? Where did this happen?"

The head teamster took over answering questions. "It happened down the road, outside of town. A bunch of men rode out of the woods, tied and blindfolded us. From the sound of them, I'm sure they were Russian. The orders and answers were in Russian. They rode up in horses and took the gold off in relays. I don't know which way they went when they left the wagon."

"What happened to the damn signal man? He was supposed to fire a shot in case of an ambush. Where the hell is he, anyway?"

Several hours later the signal man extricated himself from his bonds and report that he had been ambushed.

"Was it Finns or Russians that tied you up" asked the post commander.

"I don't know. I never knew what happened. I guess someone hit me from behind because I have a big lump on the back of my head."

The post commander said. "I suspect our own men. This same thing happened around Kiivijarvi. I think a gang of Russians grabbed the shipment of guns and ammunition, hoping the Finns would get blamed for it. They maybe just pulled off the same thing here."

The cavalry troop commander concurred saying, "The only ones that knew about the trap was us. We spread the word about the gold shipment but only a few knew about the following troop. Either it was some of our people, or we have a leak from inside our ranks. The fact that the thieves spoke Russian and knew the details of the shipment makes me think it was someone from our side."

For two futile days, the Russians tried to find some clues to the robbery and where the gold went. Patrols moved up and down the road constantly. The Finns, of course, stayed clear.

Vilho and the bunch rejoiced at the Ilta Tallo.

Vilho said, "We need to get the gold to our contact in Helsinki. Most of our supplies come from there, and the gold will be easy to dispose of there. I want it moved as soon as possible."

Waino said. "I can take it in next week on my run for supplies in Helsinki. We can make a false bottom in my supply wagon to hold the gold and bring back needed supplies the same way."

"Sounds good," said Vilho, "Now I have to get back to Kiivijarvi and see my wife and little boy. I miss them and worry about them when I'm gone."

Goodbyes were said all around, and Vilho took off for the long trek back to the cabin to see his family. Little did he know the surprise that awaited him.

Chapter Twelve

Cabin Invaders

THE CROSS COUNTRY TRIP FROM KOSKELA to Kiivijarvi, fueled by Vilho's need to get back to his family, took less time than he had planned. As Vilho neared his home, the anticipation of seeing his family grew in intensity.

From a short distance away he could see the small tree covered mesa where the cabin lay hidden. He was appalled to see a grey-white plume of smoke rising above the trees.

"Mary's being careless with the fire. She should have noticed the telltale smoke," he muttered to himself. "I'll really have to talk to her about that." But, even as he said this, he knew he was wrong. Mary and he had talked many times about smoke giving away their position. They had spent countless chilly days in the cabin when they could not build a fire because a patrol might be near. Mary would not have been that careless. Vilho knew then that something was wrong.

He moved off the trail to hide in a small clump of brush to contemplate the possibilities of what he was seeing.

"Someone's in the cabin that shouldn't be there. Mary's trying to send me a danger signal. I must proceed with caution until I find out what's wrong."

Earlier that morning Mary had been busy inside doing morning chores, and Marti was playing outside. Mary watched her active youngster from the kitchen window as she worked. He was having a fun time climbing a small tree.

She knew he couldn't hurt himself on such a small tree and he was having such a good time climbing that she let him be, knowing the worse he could get if he fell was a skinned knee. The exercise and confidence building of his effort, however, would be good for him.

Marti climbed another few feet to a crotch in the tree. He waved to his mother. The loss of one handhold while he waved made him lose his balance. He slipped and started to the ground. His leg caught at the knee and wedged in the crotch leaving him hanging upside down. It scared him, and he wailed at the top of his lungs, but he wasn't really hurt. Mary ran out to free him, but she couldn't get him loose. She couldn't reach high enough to free his wedged leg. Panic set in as Marti wailed and she struggled to set him free.

Mary ran for an ax to cut the tree down. A few strokes of the ax on the base of the slender tree started it on a slow bend toward the ground. Mary dropped the ax and grabbed her son as he got lower. With Marti at a lower level it was easier to free his leg, but he continued to wail. Mary rushed him into the cabin and held him in her arms as he sobbed for a few more minutes. She examined him closely and didn't find anything wrong. He had only been frightened. In a couple of minutes he was up and running again.

A ten-man Russian cavalry patrol, however, had been crossing the far ridge when all this was happening. The leader heard the crying and stopped the patrol.

"Listen, I swear that's a child crying over on that ridge!" said Lieutenant Prokov, the patrol leader.

"It's probably just a bobcat," said the scout. "They often sound like a crying child."

"No, I think it's actually a child. Let's investigate that ridge and see what's going on."

"If you insist, sir," said the scout, "but it's an exercise in futility. That cat will be gone before we can get close."

"Men, dismount. Corporal Malenkov, stay and watch the horses. We can't ride that narrow trail to the mesa."

The scout said, "It does look like a small trail heading that way. Some animals are using it for a high hiding place."

They came to the rock alarm and knocked the rocks clattering down the side of the ravine. Mary didn't hear the alarm because Marti was still sobbing in the cabin. The hawk left its nest, screaming in protest at the intruders, but Mary assumed it was Vilho returning as she hadn't heard the rock alarm. She managed to quiet Marti with the idea that his daddy was coming home.

The scout peeked through the trees and was surprised to see the clearing and cabin. He ducked back to stop the rest of the patrol.

"What is it? asked Prokov.

"There's a nice cabin in the clearing ahead. I think it's occupied. There's a garden and other signs of habitation."

Lieutenant Prokov said, "I'll take half the men and move up to the cabin. The other half stay here to cover us in case we come under fire. We have no cover crossing that clearing."

Mary looked up in surprise and horror to see two Russians standing in the doorway with rifles leveled at her. Marti ran to hide behind his mother. He had never seen another person other than Mary and Vilho.

Prokov snapped. "Who are you? What are you doing here?"

Mary stood closed mouthed in fear as the rest of the patrol filed into the house. One of the men said. "I believe she's Vilho's woman. I saw them together several times in town."

Prokov swung around to face Mary and demanded, "Is that true? Are you Vilho's woman?"

Mary said nothing. She hugged Marti to the back of her skirt and stared at the soldiers.

"It just came to me." said Prokov, "Colonel Tokarev was supposed to have raped her, and Vilho killed him for it."

One of the soldiers said, "I wouldn't mind trying a little of that myself."

Prokov laughed and said, "Neither would I, but I'm not sure I'd want to try unless I knew Vilho was dead."

"I'm not afraid of one Finn. I think I'll give it a try."

Mary watched the soldier approach with great fear. Marti clung even tighter to her legs. The presence of her small son finally gave her voice. "Please, not again," she whispered. "And not in front of my child."

"Wait!" said Prokov, extending his arm to block the soldier's path. "I don't want any distractions right now. We don't know where Vilho is. If something happens to him when we're trying to capture him, I'll let all of you have a go at this Finnish slut."

The scout said, "If she really is Vilho's woman and he's out hunting or something, we ought to set a trap for him right here. You know he'll come home soon with a wife and boy waiting."

"You're right, but he might not show up for days. Let's wait out the day. If he doesn't show, we'll send a messenger back to the post to let them know we're staying longer. I don't want another patrol relieving us. Think of the glory and honor we'd receive for capturing Vilho!" said Prokov.

"How shall we work it?" asked the scout.

"We have nine men, ten counting Malenkov back with the horses. We'll hide six men around the edge of the clearing. Three of us will stay inside the cabin. Vilho might bolt in any direction when he sees us. I hope we can take him by surprise but he's liable to do anything. Think of his escape from Rykov's office with four men guarding him when he leaped through a window."

The scout asked, "Do you want me to tie up the woman?"

"No, I don't think it's necessary. Even if she did call out to Vilho, he'd have to be in the clearing to hear her, and we'd have him."

The troops were placed around the clearing with great care as the Russians knew how good a woodsman Vilho was.

Mary was at her wit's end. She was relieved to have at least posponed another possible rape, but she was frantic with the idea that Vilho was sure to return that day and would walk into the Russian trap. If that happened, she had little doubt he would be killed, she would be raped, and who knew what would happen to poor Marti. She racked her brains until the idea of a smoke plume came on her.

Gathering all her courage, she asked the lieutenant, "Would it be all right if I cooked a meal for myself and my child?"

Prokov scowled at her as if conversing with her disgusted him. Finally, he dismissed her with a wave of his hand and said, "I don't care."

Mary stammered, "I . . . I'll have to get more wood. All I have in here is kindling."

The lieutenant eyes narrowed to steel. "One of my men will get the wood."

Mary swallowed. "You don't think I'd run off and leave my child, especially with all your men guarding the outside, do you?"

The lieutenant glowered. "No, I suppose not. Go ahead. I'll give you just a minute, though. If you don't come back promptly, I'll kill the child."

That idea sent shivers along Mary's spine, and she nodded mutely. She pulled Marti from her skirt and sat him down next to the stove, as far from the men as possible. He whimpered when he realized that she was leaving him, but she whispered to him and smiled that she'd be right back. Then she hurried outside and quickly gathered the greenest wood she could find and came back to light the fire.

Nervous and watchful of the men Mary set about fixing a simple meal for Marti and herself. She stoked the stove repeatedly with sticks of green wood to make sure the fire gave off thick smoke. It was the only thing she could think of to do, and she tried to make sure the fire burned all that afternoon.

Her effort paid off. Vilho saw the smoke and was forewarned of danger, but he didn't know what it was.

Vilho sat in his hiding place trying to puzzle out what he was seeing. He then carefully began to skirt the trail in the brush alongside. He eased forward cautiously expecting a trap of some kind in front of him.

He smelled the horses before he saw or heard them. A slight breeze blowing in his face told him that they were close. Horses could only mean a Russian patrol. Creeping cautiously through the underbrush, he came upon the tethered horses with the one guard. He looked around for a long time to make sure no one else lurked in hiding. The man was leaning against a fallen log, almost asleep.

Vilho crept quietly up to him, grabbed him by the hair, jerking his head back and cut his throat. Vilho sat for a minute to make sure there was no one else around to give an alarm. He rolled him out of sight behind the log.

Counting the horses he knew there were still nine men remaining. Mary's smoke alarm meant they must be at his cabin. Vilho sat trying to think of his next move against unknown circumstances.

His greatest concern was if Mary and Marti were safe. Fear for their welfare nearly filled his mind, but he forced those thoughts aside. He had to get to them, but he could not fall into a trap at the same time. He had to think. Refocused, he tried to guess what the troop commander would do to set a trap. Obviously, he had men inside the cabin, but not all nine men. The others had to be hidden around the clearing. That's what he would do, and he figured the Russian commander would be no different. That meant he could not proceed to the cabin directly. The only other way was to scale the bluff on the back side of the cabin. That way, he could get close without being seen.

Vilho hurried around as fast as he could. It was a long way around the ridge top and then down to the bottom of the bluff.

Then began the long, arduous climb to the top. The bluff was nearly perpendicular. He had to hunt hand and toe holds, taking care not to clatter rocks down and sound an alarm.

Reaching the top, he stopped to catch his breath before peering over. Through the tree trunks he thought he could see boots of a man standing at the edge of the clearing. He watched for a long time and saw the man move.

"They do have men stationed around the clearing. I wonder how many are outside and how many inside?"

Vilho knew the man whose boots he could see couldn't see him through the thicker upper foliage. He eased himself up to the flat ground and squirmed, snakelike to the back of the cabin.

Lying flat and listening intently he used his knife to pop the catch to the escape door of the sauna. He eased it open a crack to peer inside. It took his eyes a moment to adjust to the darkness inside. He could see no one in the sauna but that didn't mean no one was there, and he still didn't know how many were in the cabin. He eased the door shut and tried to think of a plan to overpower whoever might be inside.

My knife would be quiet, he thought, *but I don't know how many there are, and I couldn't get more than two before they'd shoot me. I can go in with my rifle at the ready, but I don't know where Marti and Mary are or if they'd be in danger if some one starts shooting.*

He decided he'd have to chance it with the rifle. He may be able to hear enough of their voices from the sauna to get an idea of where each one was located inside the house.

With that thought in mind, he opened the trap door and slithered inside, pushing his rifle ahead of him and at the ready in case someone stepped into the sauna.

Standing up and walking to the sauna door he listened for several minutes. He could tell where Mary and Marti; he could hear her telling him a story to calm him, and the little boy was whimpering softly. He surmised Marti was sitting on Mary's lap in the rocking chair. Several other voices murmured back and forth, but he couldn't discern their number. He could tell that at least one was walking around and one more was sitting down.

148

Vilho, with little real plan in mind, quietly pushed open the sauna door and said, "Don't anyone move even one little muscle or you're all dead."

Marti cried, "Daddy" and struggled to get free of his mother's tight grasp and run to his father, but Mary knew to hold him tight.

Prokov stood with mouth agape.

Without taking his eyes off the soldiers, Vilho said, "Mary, are you and Marti all right?"

"Yes. Fine."

"Good. Get some rawhide strips and tie the other two up and gag them.

As she did as he had asked, she nodded to one of the soldiers and said, "That one over there was going to rape me. Prokov stopped him but said if something happened to you he would let them all rape me."

Vilho felt anger rise all the way to his scalp. He glared at the lieutenant. "I ought to kill you right here and now. Fortunately for you, we have other matters that must come first. I know there are six men scattered in the trees around the cabin. I want you to call them in one by one starting with that one on the right by the corner of the cabin."

"And if I don't?

"I'll kill you and your two men here and wait until dark to go out and get the rest of your men."

"You're probably going to kill us anyway."

"No," lied Vilho, "I'll give you a chance to live if you promise not to tell of this hiding place."

Prokov licked his lips, which had dried in his fear of death. Though the idea of saving his own life pressed at him, he tried to tell himself that he was saving all his men. He nodded a curt agreement.

As the men came in one by one, Vilho and Mary bound them tightly with rawhide strips and gagged them to silence.

When they were all in the cabin and bound Prokov asked, "What are you going to do with us now?"

149

"I'm going to blindfold you, lead you far away from here and scare off your horses. By the time you get loose and find your way back to Kiivijarvi, we will have moved to a new location."

Prokov breathed a sigh of relief. It looked like his life was saved.

"Mary," instructed Vilho, "cut me some cloth strips suitable for a blindfold for each of them."

As Mary cut the strips, Vilho slipped several ghost emblems into his pocket.

Vilho tied the men one to another and blindfolded each tightly, "Move it now," he said, opening the cabin door. "Mary, start packing."

Vilho led them to the place where the horses were tethered.

"Where is Malenkov?" asked Prokov in alarm.

"He's bound and gagged behind a log," lied Vilho, "Ill get him up on one horse and tether the rest of you to his saddle."

Vilho led one horse to the front of the line and dragged Malenkov's body from its hiding place. He tied him to his horse, talked him all the while as if he were still alive. "I'm sorry you were tied up so long. I know you're stiff and sore. I'll help you up."

He tied Malenkov securely to his saddle and said to the patrol, "All right. We're ready to travel. I'll lead the horse on foot for a ways. Soon enough the horse will know which way is home and head off on its own. You'll be all right. If I catch anyone trying to peek out to get bearings, I'll kill him."

Vilho turned loose the rest of the horses and began to lead the group to within a couple of miles of town before he stopped. He walked down the line of bound soldiers, saying, "Town is just over the next couple of hills. I'm sure the horse knows the way now. I'm going to cut the ropes between you. When the horse gets to the compound a patrol will surely be sent out to find you. As I cut each of you free of the others, sit down and wait for your troops to come and rescue you.

As Vilho talked and walked down the line, he gave each man a quick knife thrust into a kidney with his blade. The rest

150

could hear only what might be a body settling quickly to the ground. Only one man made a slight grunting sound as he went down the line. When the entire patrol had been killed, he attached several ghost emblems to the men and gave the horse a slap on the rump to start it on its way to the post with Malenkov still secured to its saddle.

With this grizzly work done, he turned back to the forest and his cabin hideaway.

Mary, still looking ashen from her experience, gave a start when he entered. She relaxed when she saw it was him and said, "I'm packed and ready to leave. Where will we go?"

"We stay right here. I killed them. There really was no other choice. I attached ghost emblems to several."

"Oh, Vilho, I wish you hadn't done that. The post will be that much more determined to catch us. I hate killing, even though they are our enemy."

"Think of what they would have done to you if something had happened to me. That officer was willing to give you to his men as a diversion."

Mary swallowed. "I know you're right. Most of them acted like animals, but one of them did play gently with Marti. He said Marti reminded him of his younger brother at home."

"I would like to be at headquarters right now to see the pandemonium I have created."

Chapter Thirteen

Firing Squad

RYKOV WAS BESIDE HIMSELF THAT SOMEONE could kill that many of his men and not be accountable for it.

"It has to be the work of more than one man. How could the whole patrol be taken by surprise? It has to be Jonas leading a group. If we can track the ring leader down, we can put a stop to all this once and for all, and I can get back to Helsinki."

"Why not bring the Lehtinens in for questioning again?" suggested Gerchenoff.

"We tried that once and got nowhere. They either don't know or won't tell," sneered Rykov.

"Maybe we should apply a bit more pressure to them until they crack. I'm sure they have been helping Jonas and Vilho. They may not know where they are, but then again they just might."

"It's worth a try," conceded Rykov, "Set up a squad to pick them up."

Gerchenoff turned to the first sergeant. "I heard. I'll get it done."

The squad arrived at the Lehtinen house and knocked on the door. Anna answered.

"We have to take you and your family in for questioning at headquarters."

"You just had us a there a short time ago. We don't know anything."

"Major Rykov gave the order. Come on."

"I might have known it would be him, but I'm the only one here. My husband won't be back until late tonight, and I don't know when my son will show up."

The squad leader was in doubt as to what he should do. Picking up one older woman didn't seem fruitful, and Rykov, in the state he was in, might just dress him down. He looked to the other men for answers but got none.

"I guess I'll have to take you in by yourself."

The detail dutifully marched Anna to headquarters with the squad split in half to the front and rear as if she was some dangerous criminal.

Rykov was waiting for them in the orderly room. "Well, Mrs. Lehtinen, we meet again. I hope this time we can get some useful answers from you. Where is your husband, son, and daughter?

"My husband is working, my daughter is visiting relatives, and I'm not sure where my son is right now."

"We will deal with them when we find them. Maybe it's better this way. We'll have our own private conversation. I feel that your daughter and Jonas are somewhere together and I think you know where."

"I don't know where Jonas is, and I told you, my daughter is visiting relatives."

"There has been an incident here recently where an entire patrol was murdered by your people, and we mean to get to the bottom of it. It looks very much like the work of the resistance group, and we know that Jonas is their leader."

Anna's calm and serene manner infuriated Rykov as he normally wielded great power over all who came into his sphere. But this middle-aged woman, showed no fear, as she gazed into his eyes directly and calmly. If anything there was a little bit of contempt showing in the back of her eyes, but he couldn't be sure. He needed to find a way to make this woman talk.

Anna sat rigid as stone. She did feel contempt for the man in front of her but tried not to show it. She felt a bit of fear, knowing what this man could do to her. She had seen his temper tantrums. She wondered to herself if she could stand up to his interrogation alone; perhaps she would have to endure a beating or torture. She wished her husband could be there for help and comfort. *No,* she said to herself, *I'm glad he isn't here. He might infuriate the major again and get knocked down.*

Rykov watched for some change of emotion on Anna's face but saw none. "What makes these damn Finns so stubborn?" he muttered to himself. "I hear some word like *sisu,* but I can't believe that's all there is to it."

In a firm voice, he said, "Anna, I'm going to ask you once more where I can find Jonas. You know I can have you shot for harboring a criminal and you know Jonas was seen coming from your house."

"Women are not always told what the men are doing," she lied. "I told you before that I have no idea where he is, and I have to say that again." To herself she said, *I won't tell you anything.*

Rykov stormed out of his office and into Gerchenoff's. "That damn Finn woman is making me mad. I know she knows where Jonas is hiding, but she isn't about to tell me. I think I'll just put her up in front of a firing squad and see if she cracks then. If she doesn't I think I'd go ahead and kill her to show the townspeople I mean to get to the bottom of this killing, she just might be mistaken."

"I don't think that's a good idea," said Gerchenoff. "The people are mad enough as it is. This could stir up a local riot. We don't really have the men to fight them off if they're well organized."

"All they have is pitchforks and a few old guns. I don't see how they could put up much of a fight."

"Don't forget that shipment of new Winchesters we lost. We don't know for sure it was Russians. It could have been the Jonas group. If it was them, they'd be better armed than our troops."

Rykov scoffed. "Jonas might be smart enough to do some damage, but the rest of the townspeople are little more than angry cattle. They don't have the brains among them to organize a good attack even if they do have those guns. I'm going to assemble a firing squad. I think it will scare the woman enough to make her talk. If she does, we'll be on top of Jonas before he can act. If she doesn't talk, I just might go ahead and give the order to fire if she doesn't speak up. Personally, I think it will scare the townsfolk into obedience."

"I think that's a grave tactical error. I'm not in favor of shooting her or even threatening to do so."

"I don't give a damn what you think. I'm in command of this post, and I'll do as I damn well please."

"Then why did you come into my office for advice?"

Rykov strode back into his office without answering.

"Anna, I have given you all the chances in the world to tell me what I want to know and save your own life. I am going to order up a firing squad. If you haven't told me what I want to know soon, I'll order them to execute you."

Anna blanched. In a voice softened with fear but not weakened in resolve, she said, "I don't know what to tell you. Don't you think if I knew I would tell you?"

Rykov went to the main orderly room and ordered up a firing squad. Anna was not sure what he said as the order was in Russian, but she suspected that he was going to follow through on his threat.

Instead of breaking down, she closed her eyes and said a quiet prayer, "Lord, if it is to be that this is my last day, please accept me into your arms. I've led a good life, and I don't mind going, but I hate to leave my family. Toivo will be devastated and may do something rash and get himself killed. Please keep my son and husband safe and out of this. Amen."

Rykov led Anna out into the compound where his first sergeant had assembled the firing squad. He ordered the man to bind Anna's wrists and get a blindfold ready.

"No one wanted to do this job," the first sergeant said quietly to Rykov. "I had to give a direct order to the men to get them to obey."

Rykov made Anna stand facing the firing squad with a blindfold. He walked back to the right side of his men and gave the order, "Ready . . . aim . . . fire!"

All six rifles fired, but a weak-kneed Anna still stood facing them, her bound hands clutched at her breast.

"What the hell is the matter with you men? Can't you shoot any better than that? Again! Ready . . . aim . . . fire!"

Again the rifles spoke, but Anna did not fall.

"You damn troops can't follow a direct order. Sergeant, have these men up for court martial. Soldier, give me your rifle."

Rykov jerked the rifle out of the hands of the nearest soldier, racked a new round into the chamber, raised up and fired. Ann crumpled slowly to the ground, still clutching her breast.

His mouth suddenly dry, Rykov said, "That's how it's done. Get a cart and haul her body home to her family."

It took a little time to get a horse-drawn cart ready and load her body for transport.

"What are we going to do if her husband or son goes berserk and starts shooting at us?" asked one troop.

"We have guns. We'll shoot back," said the first sergeant.

The detail pulled up to the Lehtinen house. Toivo stood just outside, Anna's note in his hand. He wondered about the cart and where Anna was, or if they came to get him too.

The squad leader was the only one that spoke Finn and it was not very good. "We have you wife here in the cart," he said.

Toivo walked around to the back of the cart and saw Anna all covered with blood. He cried out, "My God, what have you heathens done to my wife!"

"It wasn't us," said the squad leader. "It was Major Rykov who ordered us to shoot. When we failed to hit her twice, Rykov grabbed a rifle and shot her himself. This is not what any of us wanted. We are very sorry for your loss."

Toivo overcome by grief, gently picked Anna up and carried her into the house. As he entered the door, he turned back and said, "Get off my property before I shoot you."

The squad leader slapped reins to the horse's rump and kept the horse galloping until they were well out of rifle range.

The leader breathed a sigh of relief, "I thought sure we were going to get shot."

"That damn Rykov got us into this mess," echoed one of the other men, "and it could be bloody before it's over."

Toivo carried Anna to the kitchen table and laid her down. He thought about taking her up to their bedroom, but he knew they would just have to carry her back down for burial.

"Oh, my dear Anna, what have they done to you. You don't deserve this."

Anna opened her eyes and said quietly, "Oh, Toivo, my chest hurts so bad."

Toivo started and stared, not sure he was hearing his dear wife's voice. "Thank God you're still alive."

Just then Matt came in whistling a happy tune. He stopped dead in his tracks when he saw his mother lying on the table all covered with blood.

"What happened?"

"Major Rykov shot her. She's still alive. Saddle a horse and ride for the doctor."

Matt ran for the stable and grabbed old Bessie, which was the closest thing they had to a riding horse. He didn't bother to saddle her. He just shoved a bridle into her mouth and over her ears and off he went riding bareback at a breakneck pace.

He stormed into the doctor's house and explained what happened. "Grab your satchel and ride up behind me on Bessie," he told the doctor, frantic to get back home and have his mother tended.

"No, let's take a minute to harness my horse and buggy," said the doctor. "I might need the supplies I have in there."

They literally threw the harness on his horse and had it hooked up in record time. Matt took off at a gallop with the doctor not far behind. In the yard, he leaped off and threw a hitch of the reins around the porch railing as he bounded into the house.

"The doctor is right behind me."

"I can't tell how bad she's hurt," said Toivo. "Her one hand is bleeding and all smashed up. She is bleeding badly from a hole in her chest. I'm afraid that's the bad one. I got the blood from her hand stopped some with a towel. I'm afraid she's bleeding inside. I'm surprised she has lasted this long with the jostling in that cart and everything."

The doctor came in and immediately went to work. He cut her clothes to better look at her chest wound. A second hole showed up on the side of her chest. The doctor looked puzzled and they looked through her blouse and found a spent bullet.

"It looks like the bullet didn't penetrate her chest. It hit both her hands and really damaged the left one but the right one looks all right except for the little finger. I think the bullet hit her hands from an angle and then skated along a rib to come out on her side."

"Is she going to live?" asked Toivo and Matt in unison.

"Barring any kind of infection, yes, but we have a lot of work to do on her hands, and she won't have much use of her left hand ever again. Matt, go out in the buggy and get that bottle of brandy under the seat." To Anna, the doctor said, "Anna you're going to have to drink this down in little sips."

When Matt brought the liquor, the doctor put the bottle to her lips. She took one sip and coughed, not used to the strength of the alcohol. The cough seemed to cause her a lot of pain.

"We'll have to dilute it with water so you can drink it," said the doctor. "Matt, pour half of this in another glass and fill it with water."

Anna took several sips and said, "It's still strong, but I'll drink it so you can work on me."

After a few minutes Anna was getting sleepy.

"Oh, Toivo, I feel like I'm floating on a cloud."

Her eyes closed, and she was fast asleep.

The doctor cut open the wound channel on her chest and cleaned it out. Though Anna moaned in her sleep, she never rose all the way to wakefulness as the doctor worked.

"I was right," said the doctor, "the bullet skated along her rib and came out without doing too much damage. Rykov must have been shooting from an extreme angle. We can thank God for that. One of you is going to have to assist me when I start to work on her hands."

"I'll do it," said Matt. "Father is too upset to be of much help right now."

Indeed, Toivo paced back and forth in the room, wringing his hands. Occasionally he would stop to stroke Anna's head, but the sight of all the blood soon sent him to pacing again.

"We'll work on her left hand first," the doctor said calmly and softly. "I'm going to cut the ends of the fingers off to get rid of the jagged ends. You will have to hold her hand with both hands while I saw."

Anna lost everything but the thumb and forefinger on that hand. The doctor left some flesh and skin for padding, which he sewed over the newly severed stumps. On the right hand he removed the shattered little finger entirely and sewed up the void.

"She is going to hurt in both hands and the chest for some time. Give her a little sip of watered-down brandy as needed. I'm out of laudanum right now, but I expect some in the mail tomorrow or the next day. I'll stop by tomorrow and see how she's doing."

About two hours later, Anna came out of her brandy sleep. She groaned and looked at all the bandages on her hands and asked, "What did the doctor do? It hurts so bad."

"You're going to be all right," Toivo said, giving her his bravest smile. "You lost most of your left hand, but your right one is missing only the little finger. The bullet never entered your chest. You're going to be all right. That damn Rykov is going to pay for this in kind and then some."

"Toivo, Matt promise me one thing."

"Yes, what is it?"

"Promise you won't seek revenge over this or do anything foolish that might get either one of you killed. Rykov put me in front of a firing squad and I lived. That's more than we have a right to hope for this family."

Both men promised—they would have said anything at the moment in their gratitude of knowing how close Anna came to dying and still lived—but both made up their minds that if the right chance came up, they would surely take it.

The people in town were awestruck at Anna's having lived through a firing squad and furious that the Russians could do such a thing to a woman they loved and respected. Several were for storming the compound. Fortunately, cooler heads prevailed.

Vilho came to visit as soon as he heard the news.

"Vilho, I made Toivo and Matt promise not to do anything foolish, and now I want you to give me the same promise."

"I'm a fugitive already, so if I kill him they won't do any more to me than they would do if they caught me right now."

"But, Vilho, you're like a son to me. I wouldn't want anything to happen to you because of me. Please say you won't take that chance and be killed because of me."

Vilho smiled. "I won't get killed because of you. I promise that."

Several of the people in the resistance movement came by to pay their respects and wish Anna well.

A short meeting was held later that evening at the Boar's Head, and the consensus of opinion was to wait for a more opportune time to do Rykov in. Everyone agreed that they would have to storm the compound to route Rykov out right now.

"I have to go. I can't be seen around here," said Vilho as he went out the door.

Chapter Fourteen

Vilho, Matt, and Rykov

RYKOV STAYED IN HIS QUARTERS in fear of his life after the reaction of the town to what he had done to Anna. He was sure some one from the resistance group would try to kill him. He had all his meals sent to his quarters. When he went to his office, he made sure he was surrounded by other people. His people thought it was all in his mind and that he really was not in any danger. After all, the compound was well fortified. But if Rykov had known that Vilho and Matt were trying to find some way to kill him, he would really have been worried.

Matt met Vilho secretly on the second floor of the Boar's Head in Mika's apartment. The younger man said, "What can we do to get to that damn Rykov for shooting my mother?"

Vilho shook his head. "He won't come out of his quarters and we can hardly get a shot at him there. I don't think there's any way we can get to him on the post without putting ourselves in mortal danger."

"Could we fake a message that he's to report to Helsinki? If he falls for it, we could ambush him on his way there."

"How can we get that message to him and have it look like the real thing?"

"We could get someone in headquarters to steal a letter with Golovin's signature on it and try to copy it. Golovin is still the commander in Helsinki, isn't he?"

"We can check. How do we get the letter delivered so it looks like the real thing?"

Matt considered that. "Let's find out who's on courier duty to and from Helsinki and see if we can find someone sympathetic to our cause. They use both Finns and Russians, you know."

In the course of events, they did get a copy of a letter with Golovin's signature, and they found one of their own resistance men serving on courier duty. Then, they enlisted the aid of Mika to write the letter in Russian and apply the Golovin signature.

"It will be two weeks before we can arrange everything to have the letter delivered on the courier's return trip," said Mika.

Vilho nodded. "In that case, I'm heading back home and see how Mary and Marti are getting along."

When he returned to the small cabin in the forest, Mary and Marti were happy to see Vilho. They both hugged and kissed him. Marti climbed up into his lap as soon as he sat down and chattered like a magpie about all the things he had done while his father was gone.

That night after Marti was asleep, the couple made love ever so tenderly.

Mary whispered, "It's so good to have you here and safe in my arms. I worry every time you go out that something will happen to you."

"They won't get to me. I am too careful, and I know their habits too well to get caught in any of their traps."

"I still can't help but worry. What would Marti and I do without you?"

"Not that anything is ever going to happen to me at the hands of the Russians, but I made arrangements with Mika to have him take care of both of you in case something did happen to me."

Mary settled down into his arms, and Vilho did not have the heart to tell her that he would have to leave soon and go on a mission to kill Rykov.

Vilho spent the next ten days with his family. It was hard for him to break the news to Mary and Marti when the time came close to having to return to town.

"Mary, I have to go back to Kiivijarvi on resistance business. I shouldn't be gone longer than a week or so. I'll bring back any supplies you need when I return. Please make out a list of the things you need."

As he knew she would be, Mary instantly became concerned. "Oh, Vilho, I don't want you to go. This has been such a good time with you here, and Marti just adores you. I'll miss you terribly."

"I know it's hard, and I hate to go, too, but we must make sacrifices if we are ever going to see Finland free of Russian rule."

"I know all that, and you know I want to see Finland free for Marti's sake, but it seems to me that you're doing more than your share. Can't someone else take over for you and let us live in peace or migrate to America like Jonas and Emma?"

"Maybe someday I can find someone to take my place but for now there is only me in this area."

Vilho would not admit even to himself how much he liked the intrigue and danger he faced. His adrenalin pumped high even with the thought of confronting the Russians and it gave him great satisfaction to bring them humiliation and pain.

He packed a small lunch in his rucksack and started for the door.

Marti cried. "Father, please don't go. I need you. Momma needs you. We get lonesome when you're gone."

Marti's tears almost made him turn and stay.

"Some day, Marti, you'll be old enough to understand what I am doing. If the Russians are still here when you get older, I will take you with me. Then you'll see why I have to leave."

"Take me with you now. I'm a big boy."

"Yes, you're a big boy but not quite big enough yet. Besides you have to take care of momma and keep her company."

The little boy smiled bravely and puffed out his chest.

The trip went quickly for Vilho. He was enjoying the outdoors and all that went with it, but he was still vigilant to anything that might be out of place. This trip went well, and he got to the edge of town before dark. As usual, he settled down in a clump of brush to wait. It seemed strange to him to be sitting there and watching everything moving along at its usual pace. He felt a sudden sadness well up in him thinking about the loss of freedom his people had.

"I hope the people don't get complacent and accept this life of bondage."

Darkness came, and he slipped through the shadows to the Boar's Head. Mika had finally given him a key so that he could slip up into his apartment any time he came into town.

Mika was alerted by a very small squeak of the floor as Vilho walked across it and knew the fugitive was upstairs. He told the crew he was going upstairs to eat a meal in peace and get a little rest. He fixed a plate and took it up along with a bottle of wine. This he offered to Vilho.

"The letter has been delivered," said Mika as he handed the plate of food to Vilho and opened the wine. He poured two glasses and pulled up a chair beside Vilho to talk while he ate.

"That's good. Is he going to go for it or not?"

"We have no way of knowing, and I'm sure he will balk at leaving here in the open. Rumor has it he'll probably ask Gerchenoff to provide him with a full company escort to Helsinki so he doesn't get shot. We made the letter sound urgent, so he's going to have to do something soon. If Gerchenoff refuses to give him the escort he wants, it'd be just like Rykov to try to pull rank on him. We'll have to see how it all goes."

"It sounds like Rykov's really scared."

"I know. Anyway, we should know something soon. Stay here until we hear what's going to happen."

"I hate to impose on your generosity but there isn't much point in my going back to the cabin."

"Nonsense, I just wish we could get away for a few days of fishing," grinned the tavern keeper. "Ah, such is the life of a resistance fighter. I didn't know when I got into this thing that I would be robbed of most of my free time."

"If we get our freedom, you'll have plenty of time for fishing."

They talked on into the night about all the things that were happening with the movement and plans for the future.

In the morning at headquarters, Rykov and Gerchenoff were having a heated argument.

"I outrank you, captain," Rykov said. "I can order the troops on this post anywhere I want."

"If you take a full company of men to Helsinki to protect you," said Gerchenoff, "what is Golovin going to say? I'm going to send a message to him, saying that I objected to you ordering my men away from the post just to protect your ass."

"All right!" shouted Rykov. "I'll take the men only as far as Torku. That's one day's ride from Helsinki. Then I'll return them to you. I doubt that anyone from here would go as far as Turku to try to kill me. If we don't let the Finns know when I am leaving, we may get away."

Gerchenoff shook his head. "You know that's idiotic. The Finns seem to know things before we do."

"I still insist on that full company going with me."

"That'll leave the post too unprotected. I'll agree only to a stripped-down company . . . and then only as far as Torku. One other thing. What's to keep some sniper from shooting you out of the saddle despite the men around you? You know a couple of Finns could shoot you and melt into the forest before your men could get organized for a chase."

Rykov paled. "I'll figure out some way to protect myself. You just get your company ready to go in two days," said Rykov as he stormed out of the room.

That same morning Rykov called a detail of workers into his office and outlined the plans to build a box or sort of cabin of square timbers to be affixed to a sturdy wagon. That would stop any rifle bullet, he thought. Mounted onto one of the big supply wagons, with bathroom facilities inside, Rykov felt he was insulated from a Finn attack. The only opening in the structure was a small slot the size of one timber that faced forward so he could look out, plus a short door, which was also constructed of heavy timbers, that swung forward. He would have to crawl in and out of his wooden box, but he should be safe.

One of the clerks from headquarters, a Finnish resister, brought all this information to Mika, who immediately went upstairs to discuss it with Vilho.

"This isn't good news," said Vilho. "In all probability, now we can't ambush him on the road with his bullet-proof box and the troops. We can beat them to Torku and wait for him to abandon his box and the troops."

"What makes you think he will abandon his box at Torku?" asked Mika.

"He is too much of an egotist to let Golovin know how scared he is of us Finns."

"You also mention 'we.' Who do you mean?"

"Matt Lehtinen said he wants to go. He's the only other one I want on this mission. If it weren't for Anna, I wouldn't consider him. I'd go it alone. Too many involved and someone will let the word slip or put everyone in danger. We don't want Rykov to get wind that we know his plans."

As soon as they got word of Rykov's departure, Vilho and Matt left for Torku to scout the area and look for a good place to ambush him between there and Helsinki.

Rykov was totally paranoid about getting out of his box or even showing himself while on the road. He had meals brought to him and orderlies had to empty his toilet pail. The troops snickered behind his back and made remarks about the big brave major. If Rykov heard, he made no move to stop them.

Matt and Vilho found a good spot on the road to Helsinki and set up a small camp to wait.

166

"How are we going to stop him when he comes? I'm sure he'll be riding a horse."

Vilho considered the possibilities. "We could shoot him off his horse as he rides by. We could shoot the horse and then him. We could drop a tree or rope across the road . . . if we had an ax or a rope. I remember just around the bend there, the road narrows and there are some trees and brush close to the road. We could just step out and face him. If he ran, we'd just shoot him or the horse."

A dark look came to Matt's eyes. "I personally would want him to know I'm the son of Anna before I shoot him."

Vilho regarded the young man carefully. "Matt, have you ever killed a man before?"

Matt's eyes dropped. "No." Then he lifted his chin, and the steel returned to his eyes. "I won't have any trouble doing away with this one, though."

More experienced with the ways of the world, Vilho smiled ironically. "Don't be too sure. It's a difficult thing to kill a human being. I've done it many times, as you know, but I feel bad about everyone of them, even the one who raped my wife."

They reconnoitered the area around the next corner and decided it was a good place to ambush Rykov.

"Let's pile some brush on the right side of the road so he'll have to go close to the trees on the other side. We can step out from behind the trees and grab the reins," said Matt.

Vilho agreed. "We can both hide behind those big trees. Well be on him before he knows it."

"We can watch him approach from the curve. When he starts down this long straight stretch, we'll still have plenty of time to get into position."

"Let's cut some brush now, but we better not put it in the road until we see him. Someone else may come along and report the suspicious pile or move it out of the way. I don't think he'll be here until tomorrow anyway. We made a lot better time than that top-heavy wagon of his and that escort train."

167

They cut the brush and laid it out so they could move it quickly into the road. They made themselves a comfortable camp and prepared to wait. Neither one of them slept very well, however. Vilho worried how Matt would perform, and Matt worried about his own abilities. Mostly Matt worried about having to kill a man.

At early daylight, Vilho roused and said, "Matt, you watch the road toward Torku while I fix some breakfast. I don't think he'll be here for some time yet, but he might surprise us with an early start."

Rykov didn't show early. The two Finns cleaned up after breakfast and put out the small fire. They sat cross legged on a little knoll overlooking the road, taking turns with the telescope. Matt had just taken the telescope when he spotted a lone rider. He put the scope to his eye and said in a whisper, "It's him."

Vilho took the scope to verify and announced, "You're right. It's him in the flesh. Let's get ready."

They slid the brush down the bank to effectively block most of the road. Vilho took the tree nearest the road, and Matt stood just a little ways further back.

Rykov rode up, unconcerned, looked askance slightly at the pile of brush as he started around it. Vilho stepped out and grabbed the horse's reins. Rykov panicked when he recognized Vilho and spurred the mount. The horse unable to proceed with Vilho still holding the reins reared. Rykov slid off the back of the horse, and Vilho let the reins go. The horse walked off a few paces with the reins dragging.

"Get up, you Russian pig," Vilho commanded.

Rykov sat up blinking and said, "Please don't kill me. I'm on my way to Helsinki. I'll never be back in your territory again."

Matt emerged from the woods at that moment, and Rykov swiveled his head to look at the younger man, recognizing him from interrogation sessions. The Russian then fixed his eyes on the American rifle Matt held at the ready. He knew he had little hope as he turned pleading eyes to Vilho.

"You shot my mother who never hurt a soul in her life," hissed Matt. "She is still alive thanks to God."

"She wouldn't tell me where Jonas and Vilho here were hiding. I'm sure she knew."

"She didn't know. Even if she had, she wouldn't have told you. Unlike you, you whimpering pig, she had the heart of a warrior. She was ready to die for Finnish freedom even when you threatened her with death."

"Please don't kill me," pleaded Rykov. "I'm sorry I shot her and . . . I'll never hurt another Finn in my life."

"Shoot the damn liar," said Vilho in disgust.

Matt raised his rifle, cocked the hammer and paused for a moment. His jaw tightened repeatedly and the tip of the rifle wavered. Finally, he lowered the weapon and looked at Vilho. "I can't do it. You'll have to do it."

"It was your mother he shot."

"Maybe we can shoot his hands off like mother's and let him go on to Helsinki."

"He'd be able to identify you."

Matt drew in a long breath. "There's no other way, is there?"

Vilho shook his head. "There is only the way to freedom."

Matt raised the rifle again, drew it carefully on Rykov and shot him full in the chest. With a look of terror and surprise, Rykov fell backwards with his arms out flung. Matt turned around and vomited.

"It's all right, Matt," said Vilho gently. "I did the same thing the first time I killed someone."

Vilho went through Rykov's pockets, taking his money, his pocket watch, and a ring from his finger.

"What are you doing?" asked Matt incredulously. "Let's just get out of here."

"I'm making this look like a robbery, but I'm also going to leave a ghost emblem for the Russians to find."

They gathered up their gear and started the long trek back to Kiivijarvi.

Chapter Fifteen

Helsinki Response

RYKOV'S BODY WAS DISCOVERED the next morning by a Finnish farmer. At first the simple man was afraid to report it for fear the Russians might blame him. Local authorities did question him, but he was soon released.

The Russians transported Rykov's body to Helsinki for examination and burial. The examiners reported that he was shot point blank in the chest and the bullet went clear through. Golovin was disappointed that they couldn't tell him more. Shortly afterwards, Golovin called a meeting of his staff to discuss the death of Rykov.

"What I don't understand is why he was on the road in the first place. He was supposed to be in Kiivijarvi trying to hunt down those damn Finnish renegades. Is it possible he was killed elsewhere or captured elsewhere and brought to that spot for killing?"

"I don't think so," replied Kalashnikov, one of his trusted staff. "He lay in a pool of his own blood. It's possible that he was captured elsewhere, but then I don't see the significance of killing him on the road. I think he was coming to Helsinki, and we need to find out why."

Leslie W. Wisuri

Golovin jumped up from behind his desk, paced the floor and sat down, only to bounce back up and pace some more. He grabbed his pipe and stuffed it full and then threw it back down on his desk, scattering tobacco shreds everywhere.

"Major Kalashnivov, send a rider to Kiivijarvi to find out why Rykov was on his way here," said Golovin as he started pacing the room again. There's no use trying to figure out what happened until we hear why he was coming here. Dismissed."

"The colonel is in a bad mood," remarked one of the departing staff.

"You would be too if you had the tsar breathing down your neck. I mean, we're talking about one or two renegades and not the entire Finnish population. In my mind, everyone would be better off if we ignored the whole damn thing."

"They are afraid this will lead to more dissent and resistance . . . maybe a complete breakdown of our rule over Finland."

"I hardly think two men could do that."

The rider arrived in Kiivijarvi, inquiring about Rykov's mission. Word got back to Mika. Gerchenoff would find out that Golovin hadn't sent a letter ordering Rykov to report to Helsinki. That would put the courier who had delivered the spurious letter at serious risk.

Vilho came into Mika's that same night. After closing Mika went upstairs, and he and Vilho had a long talk.

"I think we ought to contact him right away. They're liable to pick him up, and I'm not sure how he'd stand up under questioning. He could give away most of our operation in this area," said Vilho.

"I don't think so," said Mike. "You're the only one who contacted him in any way, and you're already a hunted man. What are we going to say to him when he gets here?"

"I want to thank him personally for delivering the letter and apologize for putting him in jeopardy. We'll see what he wants to do. I have several ideas to solve the problem, but I don't know if he's willing. Until we know for sure where he stands let's not get you involved in any way."

171

"We can't let one of our own be taken by the Russians for such a minor offense," rejoined Mika.

"No, we can't. Let's send word for him to meet here at the Boar's Head."

Tauno Kalio, the courier, came in that evening. He was upset when he found out about the course of events and how it could affect him.

"I'm for freedom like you, but here I'm in the middle of it for a simple little job of delivering a letter."

"I've given this a lot of thought," said Vilho, patting him on the shoulder. "I think it best you go away from here to some other outpost and reenlist. You're young enough to make them think you're just now turning of age. We'll have to get some false papers and maybe change your name. If there's a resistance movement in the area of your choice, we'll see to it that they welcome you with open arms. We'll send them the information on what you've done."

"I don't know . . . I have a life started here."

"If you stay here, they'll make you talk, and then they'll kill you as a traitor."

"What will I tell my family and friends?"

"Explain the situation. Tell them this won't be forever as we will gain our freedom soon, and you'll come back a hero."

That last idea caught Tauno's imagination. He left the next day for an outpost in the far north. Headquarters put out a search for him that same morning. Also that same morning, Gerchenoff sent the message back to Helsinki about Rykov's false letter.

Golovin called another meeting as soon as he read the message from Kiivijarvi. None of his men were looking forward to this meeting as the news was already out, and Golovin was furious. The courier gave everyone the news about the fake letter.

"We have talked of this before," said Golovin. "I'm at my wit's end what to do about these damn Finn renegades. This time I'm sure it was the Finns, too. Some of the other raids could be

172

blamed on them or possibly our own people, but this reeks of revenge for the shooting of that housewife. I don't know what got into that man to do such a thing. Our relationship with the Finns is getting worse and worse. Stupid mistakes like this do not help."

An uneasy silence fell over the room. No one had any idea what to do, and they knew Golovin was going to continue his babble about hunting down the enemy. Each man shifted in his chair, some coughed, and others looked blankly at the ceiling.

"This is definitely the work of the Finns," said Golovin as if convincing himself. "I see no reason why anyone else would kill Rykov. He was a hard task master, but I doubt if any soldier hated him enough to kill him. After all it's the duty of a soldier to follow orders even though they may seem harsh and unjust."

Kalashnikov cleared his throat and said softly, "I understand they found one of the ghost emblems by his body."

Golovin's eyes met his. "Yes, they did. This makes me think it was the work of Finns from the Kiivijarvi area."

"Might this have been a direct diversion to throw suspicion on to the Finns? I heard that this happened on some raids that looked like the Finns but may have been some of our own men trying to make some extra money."

Golovin grew irritated. "We are going to need a replacement for Rykov at the Kiivijarvi outpost. Major Kalashnikov, with all your interest in this deed, you might be just the man we need as a replacement."

Kalashnikov swallowed. The last thing he wanted was to be put in charge of the mess at Kiivijarvi.

Golovin droned on for another half hour before dismissing the bored men. The next morning he called Kalashnikov into his office. "Major, using you as the replacement for Rykov has jelled during the night. It's a good idea. I'm going to send you there to take care of this business. You can pick up to six men to go with you. I would expect you to take your own orderly and whatever staff people you think you might need up there to bring order to the region and bring the perpetrators of this violence to justice."

"Sir, surely there are more competent people we could send. Maybe we don't need to replace Rykov at all, Gerchenoff seems to be doing a good enough job."

"Good enough job? Hell he hasn't caught that damn Jonas in five years, and now they have a second renegade by the name of Vilho loose up there, and they haven't been able to lay a hand on him either. Pretty soon the whole damn region will be full of renegades."

"What makes you think I can do any better than Rykov or Gerchenoff?"

"Maybe some fresh thinking on the subject will get some results."

Try as he might Kalashnikov could not sway Golovin from sending him to Kiivijarvi.

Three days later Kalashnikov and his entourage left Helsinki for the post in Kiivijarvi.

Gerchenoff received him cordially enough but wrote him off as another damn know-it-all from headquarters going to interrupt his routine.

Chapter Sixteen

Kalashnikov

KALASHNIKOV SETTLED RELUCTANTLY INTO HIS QUARTERS, but he got his staff working in Rykov's old office in short order. As soon as he got settled he went into Gerchenoff's office to talk.

"Captain, I'm not here to interrupt or change your routine, at least not yet. I'm going to snoop around and observe everything here on the post and in town before I make any changes. I may not change anything at all. In any case I'll discuss the possibilities with you when I know them."

"I appreciate that, sir," said Gerchenoff. "We do have a smooth operation going on here when the Finnish renegades don't disrupt our training schedule. There are the extra troops billeted here at your disposal for the purpose of running them to ground. Personally, I think we ought to forget them and go on about our business."

Kalashnikov said, "On the surface of things I think you're right. The whole thing started with such a minor incident. A public whipping and the accidental killing of a Russian officer. I've read the reports. All could have been smoothed over long ago. Not now. There's been so much loss of face that I doubt either side can find a stopping place. And now we have the second renegade and reports of some uprisings in other communities. We could lose all of Finland over the whipping of one man for a minor offense. How tragic."

"These Finns have always had a fierce yearning for freedom. I'm not so sure the whipping and subsequent killings amount to all that much in the face of the desire for freedom. These few incidents here just brought a lot of it to the surface. Now though, many other Finns have seen what a few were able to accomplish, and it's given them the courage to take up the challenge. That's where the real danger lies."

"I'm sure you're right, but there isn't much we can do about the beginnings of all this. We have to deal with what we face now."

"We keep trying, but it seems to be getting harder and harder to control them."

Kalashnikov nodded. "That's going to be my main job, difficult as it is. Right now, though, my belly is telling me to eat. Is there a place to eat off the post? Are there any good restaurants in the area?"

"It's a small town," said Gerchenoff, "and there's really only the one, but it serves quite good food. Go to Mika's Boar's Head. Anyone in town can direct you to it."

"We have a Boar's Head in Helsinki with excellent food."

"That was the original place. Mika sold out in Helsinki and came up here because he likes to fish. We gained an excellent restaurant for that reason."

"Well, I'll give it a try. We'll talk later."

Kalashnikov strode into the Boar's Head and introduced himself to Mika. "I'm Rykov's replacement. I'm not sure if that's a good thing or not. I understand Rykov was a bit of a tyrant."

"So some people say," said Mika noncommittally.

Kalashnikov tried to draw Mika into conversation several times, but Mika seemed suspicious and reserved. Kalashnikov wondered, *I wonder what it takes to get next to this man? I think he'd be a great ally in creating a more peaceful atmosphere around here if I can get him on my side.*

Kalashnikov ordered steak with some misgivings, knowing how tough some rural beef could be, but when he tasted his meal, he was amazed at how good everything was. "I can't imagine such a fine restaurant as this off in the hinterlands," he raved to Mika. "You should be serving heads of state in Helsinki, St. Petersburg, or Paris. I'm going to have to eat here often."

By his third trip to the restaurant in as many days, Mika decided in the back of his mind that this man was not another Rykov. His distrust of the Russians still held sway, but he did give ground grudgingly.

"That was a great meal, Mika," said Kalashnikov with a satisfied sigh. "Let me buy you a drink in appreciation and bring me a brandy."

Mika returned to the table with two brandy snifters and the bottle. With a little hesitation, he sat down. *Damn it,* he thought, *I like a man that appreciates good food. He can't be all bad if he has some appreciation of the better things in life.*

They each sipped their brandy and eyed each other, wondering what the next topic of conversation should be. Mika wanted to question him on what he was going to do in the area, and Kalashnikov wanted to question Mika on what to do to better relations.

Kalashnikov took the risk and began first. "Mika, you seem to be a man who has a pulse on what's going on in the area. All wise tavern owners I've known do. What can I do to make things runs more smoothly between my people and you Finns?"

Mika wouldn't be drawn into reckless conversation so easily. "Are you serious, or are you just making idle conversation after a good meal?"

"I am serious," said Kalashnikov, with an expression of true sincerity.

Mika began slowly. "There are many grievances . . . mostly, at least to many of us Finns, because of the heavy-handed way you treat us. Your people confiscate livestock and grain, giving almost worthless scrip in return and, even at full value, they never pay enough."

Kalashnikov leaned on the table. "Give me some instances, some details."

Mika spread open his hand, thinking. "The widow Leppanen has five children to raise after her husband was killed in one of your military exercises. She was not in any way compensated for her loss. Then you took her one and only milk cow, a dozen chickens, and two pigs. The scrip she received in payment for these animals wasn't even enough to buy one poor cow, let alone everything else taken from her. She has had to rely on the charity of her neighbors to feed her children. That's difficult for a proud Finnish woman to do."

"How did her husband die?"

"He was shot while working in his own garden in his own yard. Your people had some kind of field exercise going, but the shooting was supposed to be away from town. We heard rumors that some soldiers dared another to shoot him, and he did. Shot him as unfeelingly as a can off a stump. That unit was completely Russian. If there had been any Finnish enlisted men with them they would have stopped it . . . at the cost of their own lives, if necessary. Your high command denied the whole thing, saying anyone could have shot him."

Kalashnikov frowned and sat back. "I'll see what I can do."

"I have dozens more of the same kinds of mistreatment. It's only through the natural good nature of us Finns that any of you Russians still live."

Kalashnikov left leaving Mika with mixed feelings. He wondered if the new officer really meant to do something or was just talking, fishing for information to use against him at some later date.

Vilho came by that evening, and they talked long into the night about how the movement was going and this latest development in the post command.

Vilho finally said, "I can hear you saying in a round about way that this Kalishnikov might be good for us, but I'll never be able to trust any Russians. I never thought you could either. The risk of doing so is enormous."

"What about Yuri Yanov? He's proven himself an asset to our group."

"I'll give you that . . . but only so far. He's been good for us, and I kind of like the man even if he is Russian, but I find myself still waiting for the other shoe to fall."

"Let's wait and see if he continues to help before we condemn him."

"I'm not going to hold my breath."

Kalashnikov continued his observations and talked with Mika several times about Russians mistreating Finns. After several weeks of checking stories back and forth he went to talk with Gerchenoff.

"Captain, I've been doing some snooping and asking a lot of questions. It looks to me like we've been treating the Finns badly."

Gerchenoff cocked and eyebrow at him. "In what way?"

"Almost any way you can name. We confiscate livestock, grain, or anything else that suits our fancy, and we pay them too little in scrip that they have a hard time spending."

"They are, after all, a defeated country," observed Gerchenoff. "Why shouldn't we be able to take what we want?"

"Well, you see, it's not quite true that Finland is a defeated country. It's a Grand Duchy and, as such, has some amount of home rule, although we haven't allowed them any chance at self-rule."

Now Gerchenoff frowned. "If you give these damn Finns an inch, they'll take a mile and then some."

Kalashnikov nodded almost in sympathy. "I'm going to opt for an easier rule. Starting now, some gross injustices will be corrected. The first one is the situation of the Leppanen widow. She's been dealt with very badly, and, from what I've learned, mostly at our hands. See to it that she gets the livestock replaced—good livestock. I'll see what I can do to get her some compensation for us shooting her husband. Tomorrow I'll have a list of other situations that I want rectified. I'm sure I haven't uncovered a complete list, but we'll make a start."

Gerchenoff grumbled to the first sergeant after Kalashnikov left, "That nobleman is going to coddle those damn Finns to the point where they'll think they can do anything,"

"He does seem to have a lot of sympathy toward them."

"That may be to his detriment at some point."

Vilho showed up at Mika's and tiptoed upstairs. Mika knew he was up there by the squeaking of floor boards and knew he wanted to talk soon by the frequency of that tiny noise. He, himself, was anxious to talk to Vilho about the latest with Kalashnikov. He shooed everyone out of the restaurant early and went upstairs.

"Greetings, you wanderer of the hinter lands," said Mika expansively. "How does your family stand it with you being away so much?"

Vilho grinned. "Greeting to you, oh great chef. My family does get a little put out with me being gone so much, but they understand how important our freedom is to all of us."

"I want to talk to you about the new officer from Helsinki. This Kalashnikov has done a lot to relieve the tension between our two peoples. I hope this doesn't make everyone so complacent that they no longer want freedom. I know if this keeps up it's going to be harder to recruit people into the movement."

"The Finnish people want freedom too much to let this bother their quest. It's a separate thing from equity of rule. Sure, there's going to be a few that are too lazy or too scared to do anything that might jeopardize what they have now."

"We'll have to watch what he does in the future. One good deed does not make him a hero, but clearly he's improving tensions."

Kalashnikov became such a regular at Mika's that the few times he failed to show up Mika wondered about him. Over brandy one night, he talked about his personal life for the first time.

"I like and admire you Finns," he said, clapping Mika on the back, "and I can see why you want freedom from us. Mother

Russia is not always considerate of her possessions. It is difficult to convey to the tsar how things are out in the field. I did not understand a lot of it until I came to Finland and saw things first hand. I admit to having personally gone along with a lot of things that might cause St. Petersburg to frown. I have become addicted to your sauna ritual. It's wonderful. We don't have anything like that back in Russia. I have always liked to keep clean, which might be more than I can say for a lot my fellow countrymen, and the sauna feels so very clean."

Mika smiled. "I've noticed those Russians who don't use the sauna, especially inside in the winter time. The sauna is an important part of our life. Finns believe that cleanliness is next Godliness. In most marriages, the couple builds a sauna before they build a house. Many have lived a few years in the sauna while they accumulated enough money to build a house."

For a moment Kalashnikov was quiet. Then he said, "You haven't made any comments on the progress we've made in our relationship with the townsfolk. Are we doing a good job or not?"

"Thus far you have done a lot of things. You have made more progress in a couple of months than Rykov did in five years. We do appreciate the lessening of tensions. That's not enjoyable for anyone. It would be a mistake in thinking, though, if you were to believe that you can kill our drive for freedom. One day we shall have it. I don't know when or how, but one day Finland will be free."

"You may be right. There's been some discussion back in St. Petersburg that this whole occupation is costing too much money for what we are getting out of it. Right now there's almost as much unrest in Russia as here in Finland for the tsar to worry about. He wants to simplify his rule and consolidate more of the people and keep them loyal to him."

This was good news to hear. "Well, you can understand that we would take full advantage of getting our freedom if something happened in Russia to interrupt the status quo."

Kalashnikov grinned. "I guess I'd do that very thing."

They talked again many times, and Mika got a sense that Kalashnikov was a good man. He might even turn to Finland's side in the event that Russian treatment of Finns worsened. He might even opt for becoming a real Finn.

Mika conveyed his thoughts to Vilho on his next stopover.

"Mika, you might trust him, but he is Russian and I'm one who's always going to be suspicious of them. He has done some good, and I'm glad for it—even righted some terrible wrongs. He's made living with them a bit more tolerable, but he hasn't changed the fact that they are still our rulers and we are still not free."

"I know that. I can't ever forget that, but I see no harm in cultivating the goodwill of a good man, though Russian. He can do more good than harm if we keep him happy and headed in the right direction."

Chapter Seventeen

Marti

VILHO CAME HOME TO HIS FAMILY and the usual boisterous reception from his son.

That night after Marti was asleep Mary got serious about his education. "I can't really teach him any more. It's time he went to a real school. My Aunt Tekla would be glad to take him in. No one knows he is our son. She could say he is the son of her sister who was killed along with her husband in a wagon accident, or died of the plague or some other plausible thing."

"I didn't have much schooling, and I know I'm ignorant about a lot of things. Maybe you're right."

In the morning they told Marti about their plans for him to live in town and go to school.

"I don't want to go into town and live," the boy said firmly. "I want to stay here with you. You said I was needed here to keep mamma company when you're gone."

"I know but you need to learn so many more things than I can teach you. You'll meet other kids your age and have fun. You'll have so much fun in school. This is the only life you know right now. There is a great big world out there for you to see."

"You don't have to go right now," said Mary quickly. "The three of us will go into town and meet Tekla and see if she'll keep you. If she agrees, we'll come and visit as often as we can. Then you'll have the whole summer here at the cabin."

Marti sulked until time to go into town. They worried about his entering a strange new world.

Tekla agreed readily to taking Marti. Marti liked her and voiced his opinion that he could take it as long as they came to visit often.

They went back to the cabin and prepared for a summer of fun. Vilho planned to spend as much time as possible with Marti and Mary, fishing and having fun together. Still fall came all too soon.

Vilho sat Marti down for a serious talk. "I know it's hard for you to understand right now about getting some education. Some day all the work we are doing against the Russians may set us free. If this country does gain its freedom, there'll have to be educated people ready to take over and run the country. You'll need to be a part of that, but you need to learn how to do all the things for freedom other than fighting."

"I just want to go with you to fight the Russians now."

"You can do more for your country by being ready to help run it when we get our freedom, and I know we'll get it. Study America and how they have done things to become a great nation."

"That doesn't sound as exciting as fighting the Russians like you do."

"It'll be a lot more satisfying and to be able to run the country well or at least have a part in it."

Marti felt a little better about going into town, but his heart still wanted to be with his father in the thick of things.

Tekla took him to school and explained to the teacher that his mother had been a teacher and had taught him at home.

"His father was killed in a hunting accident before he and his mother could get married so he has our family name Kusjarvi. They lived on a remote farm with her parents. She died of pneumonia. It was agreed a long time ago that I would take him if anything happened to her. You'll have to test him to put him in the right grade, but his mother said he would be in the fourth grade the last time I talked to her, which was about a month ago."

Marti got along well in school. The teacher came to see Tekla one evening after school. She said, "Marti is doing very well in school. He's bright and eager to learn. I think he should really be in the fifth grade. I think he gets bored with some of our material at times. He sits and looks off into space as if day-dreaming, but when I call on him he has the answers. The only reason I hesitate to put him in the fifth grade is that he would be with much older kids, and he could get teased or picked on. Right now he is having some problems with a couple of boys in his class that are teasing him because he is so smart."

"I'll leave it up to you," said Teckla. "You're with him every day in class and can make a decision better than I. It looks to me like he should go up to the next level if he is capable even though he might be with bigger kids."

"I'll give him a few more weeks in this grade before I make my decision."

"I thank you for coming and telling me how he's doing. Please feel free to call any time."

"Yes, I will."

Marti's schooling went well until one of the boys who had been teasing him started in about him not having a father. This turned out to be a sore spot with Marti, and the Keski boy exploited it even further.

"You're a bastard kid. You don't even know who your father was for sure. You don't belong among us decent people."

Marti was nearly in tears from the constant teasing of his fellow schoolmate. He blurted out, I know who my father is and he's alive. He's Vilho Maki, a freedom fighter and the best friend of Jonas the Ghost."

"I don't believe you. You're making that up because you're ashamed of not having a real father."

With that Marti pounced on him, got him to the ground and bloodied his nose before the teacher could separate them.

Marti realized he made a major mistake. He took off running for Tekla's house. He burst into the living room all out of breath. "I let the secret out," he said between great gulps of air and sobs, "I told Reino Keski who my real father is. I couldn't help it. I was mad about him calling me names and saying I didn't have a father. I better head for the cabin before some Russians come to pick me up."

"Don't get in a hurry. They probably won't believe you anyway."

Ivar Keski came over with his son late that evening wanting an apology but more to find out if Marti was telling the truth. That kind of information would be worth a lot, and Ivar was an informant of sorts.

"I want an apology from your boy," he said roughly to Tekla. "I also want him to tell my son it's a lie that he's the son of Vilho Maki."

"I don't know what got into the boy," said Tekla apologetically. "He was being defensive about not having a father and said that because Vilho is a kind of hero."

"Vilho's not any kind of a hero. All he's really done is disrupt our relations with Russia. Where's the boy? I want to talk to him."

"He's in his room and won't come out. Your son has been teasing him ever since he got here, and I think it's your son who owes Marti an apology."

With that Ivar grabbed his son by the arm and stormed out of the house.

"He's gone," said Tekla, peeking out the window. "You can come out."

Marti also looked out the window. "I think he's going to turn me in to the Russians. Now I'm sure I must go back to the cabin."

"I think you're right. Do you think you can find your way back by yourself?"

186

"I think so," said Marti without much conviction in his voice.

"I'll fix you some lunch tonight for the trip, and you can get an early start in the morning. Right now I'm going to the Boar's Head and leave word with Mika in case your father shows up. You'll be all right until I come back."

Marti took off early in the morning with very little confidence. He had been over this route only twice in his life going and coming from Tekla's, and he hadn't paid as close attention to detail as he now wished he had.

Ivar did indeed go to Russian headquarters with the news.

Gerchenoff took the report quite casually, saying, "I doubt that this is Vilho's kid. I didn't know he was married unless he married that Mary Peponen who claimed she was raped by that engineer. It'd be funny if the boy is Mary's. He might be half Russian."

"I've seen the incident report on the rape. From what Ivar said, Marti is the same age as my boy. He would have to be six or seven months older for him to be the result of the rape."

"Maybe we ought to bring the boy in for questioning. First sergeant, send a patrol down there and bring that boy back here along with his aunt or whatever she is to that boy."

The squad went to Tekla's house. She acted surprised and went to Marti's room.

"He isn't here. I can only imagine that he left last night or early this morning to go back to his grandparents."

The squad reported back empty handed.

"Where the hell is the kid and the woman?" roared Gerchenoff, "I told you to bring them both in."

"He's gone. The woman thinks he went back to his grandparents because he was so embarrassed about the lie and the fight. She said she's going to go there to find him."

Tekla packed up her meager belongings and left for Koskela where she knew some other people in the resistance. Better that than becoming a prisoner and facing a firing squad the way Anna had. She couldn't afford to trust that the Russians would treat her in any other way.

Just before daylight, Mika heard a soft knock on his door. He got up and let Vilho in.

Mika told him what happened to his son. Vilho thanked him and took off for the cabin.

"If something happens to that boy, I'll never forgive myself nor will Mary ever forgive me."

Well on the trail to the cabin, Vilho spotted some movement ahead of him. His telescope told him it was his son. He decided there was no immediate danger. He thought perhaps it would be good to see if the boy could find his way home and not panic.

Marti found the trail just fine and had a reunion with his mother. He was not quite through telling her all the details when Vilho walked in.

"You did a fine job finding your way, son. I followed you from the lake. I got word from Mika what happened just about the time you were leaving for here."

"I'm glad I'm out of that dumb school."

"Don't be too sure young man. We're going to find you some other school for you to attend. Maybe this time you can keep your mouth closed when you get angry."

Chapter Eighteen

To Koskela

TEKLA MOVED TO KOSKELA to be out of the way of the people in Kiivijarvi inquiring about Marti. She heard from Vilho that things were getting a little easier since Kalashnikov took over, but she had seen Anna's hands.

Vilho and Mary thought it would be safe to enter Marti in the Koskela school under the same circumstances as in Kiivijarvi. They agreed that it would be best if they not mention his schooling in Kiivijarvi at all. Marti was all for staying at home or joining his father in forays on the Russians, but, after freedom, education was closest to a Finn's heart.

"Young man, someday you'll realize how important your education is not only to you but to our country. The fighting I'm doing is fine, but when we get our independence, I don't have the education to run anything. We need people like you to take over that responsibility."

"But, father, it may take years to get our independence and I feel like I haven't done anything to help."

"When you finish high school, I'll let you come with me on some missions. After that I want you to attend college in Helsinki and study government."

189

"That would mean four more years of school. I don't know if I want to do that."

"Well, maybe later you'll have more interest in going to college and learning more about how this world operates."

"I doubt that, but I'll go to school as you want. I like Aunt Tekla, and I don't mind staying with her."

The three of them made a trip to Koskela to enroll Marti in the fall term even though it was spring. They planned another idyllic summer together back at the cabin. It turned out Marti's teacher was a member of the resistance and promised to keep him safe from harm and would try to get him out of trouble before he lost his temper again.

Vilho got his teacher aside and said, "Marti needs to be taught how important it is for him to become educated. I want him to go to college so he can help govern this country if and when we gain our independence."

"I'll do that. Not many people are as forward looking as you are. I'm with you in that respect. We need to think ahead to what will happen when we do gain our freedom. If we're not prepared, some other nation will take freedom away from us again."

The next morning they left for the cabin. On the way, Vilho pointed out markers on the trail that the Russians would not notice.

"If you get in trouble, and I hope you don't, this trail will lead you back to the cabin and us. The Russians seldom come this way because it's too hard for their horses. This trail is narrow so you can step off and hide quickly if you do hear someone coming."

"What if I don't hear them coming?"

"That's something I will teach you this summer: how to detect strangers in the forest before you ever see them. I hope by the end of summer this will be a part of you. If you do come upon a horse patrol, you should run like crazy through the brush. They can't follow you on horseback, and few of those Cossacks will dismount to chase you. Even if they did dismount, you and your young legs could outrun them. Remember, if this happens, you must lead them away from the cabin. They might bring in dogs to track you. I'll give you a supply of pepper to dust your trail if you are pursued. The pepper will make the dogs lose your scent."

"It looks like I have a lot to learn. Maybe I should just stay in the woods until I learn it all."

"You have a lot to learn. I can teach you about the woods and fighting, but I can't teach you about running the country. You have to learn from experts who know as much about government as I do about the woods."

They spent the summer together. The three of them went on many outings to fish and pick berries. Two near encounters with Russian patrols taught Marti the rudiments of listening to the forest sounds. These subtle changes send the warning of danger approaching.

It was time to go to Koskela for the start of school. Marti still did not want to leave, but Vilho and Mary talked him into going. Mary wasn't going to go with them at first, but Marti wanted her to accompany them so he could be with her a little longer. Mary gave in, saying she had some shopping to do in Koskela.

Vilho left Marti and Mary at Teklas' and went to see about the resistance movement. He entered the Ilta Tallo tavern and was greeted warmly by Waino Koski and Yuri Yanov. Yuri was brimming with news. "Vilho, it's coming," he said excitedly. "Freedom for Finland. There's much unrest in Russia. The talk is that there'll be a revolution to oust the tsar. Many factions are fighting for power. I think they'll oust the tsar and then fight amongst themselves. This will be good for Finland. None of the parties will have time to think about this country."

"I hope you're right, Yuri. It also means that we have to be prepared to take over the government. We'll have to write our own constitution and spell out how we want the country run."

"I have relatives back in Russia in groups like we have here. They too, want to get rid of the tsar. From everything I hear I

191

want to be with your kind of government when all this happens. It's a lot safer than what Russia will be like with so many vying for power."

Waino broke in, saying, "I hear the same kind of rumors here in the tavern. That old saying, where there's smoke there's fire. We have to keep up the pressure so that whoever comes into power in Russia will not want to take on us stubborn Finns."

"I agree. We ought to step up our raids on their supply trains now. We can take that food and give it to the ones the Russians have robbed."

They talked, formulating plans for increased harassment of the Russians.

Vilho broke it up saying, "I have to go see how my son is settling in for school. He wants to join in the fight so much, but I want him to get an education even more."

Vilho walked in while Tekla and Marti were gabbing like long-lost friends even though it had only been a few months since they had seen each other.

"We got Marti enrolled in the fifth grade," Tekla told Vilho. "The teacher gave him some tests, and he passed fine for the fifth grade. The teacher said he could almost make it for he sixth, he was so good," said Tekla proudly.

Vilho and Mary left for the cabin after some tearful goodbyes and an admonishment to Marti to keep his temper in check and his mouth closed.

Marti loved school in Koskela. He and Tekla got along well together. Marti also found out about girls. He did not know what was happening, but he had a crush on a girl named Lilia. She was slim, blonde and blue eyed. Her hair was cut short, giving her a boyish look. Marti would sneak looks at her when she wasn't looking. She was doing the same thing. Their romance, however, was slow to blossom. A gutsy girl, she liked to play with the boys in their games even tough some were rough and tumble. Lilia and Marti had body contact in some of their sports. Every time they did, they looked into each other eyes. The body contacts became more often. In a game of hide and seek, they both hid in a shed. Marti kissed her on the cheek and then fled in embarrassment.

When Lilia caught up with him, she whispered, "Why did you run away? I wanted to kiss you back."

"I was afraid you might slap my face or something."

"I would never slap your face unless you did something really bad. I don't think kissing is bad."

They became inseparable, going everywhere hand in hand. Some of the bully boys were jealous because Lilia was such a beautiful girl. An encounter came about that could have led to a fight but was stopped by the teacher who saw the potential for disaster. The boys then started calling Marti the teacher's pet, but he managed to ignore their remarks through clenched teeth and fists.

Marti helped one of the bully boys with some math problems and thus gained the favor of the rest of them. Marti's enthusiasm for freedom was contagious, and students formed a youth group for freedom with Marti as the leader. The teacher was amazed at how Marti turned the situation with the bullies around and was now their acknowledged leader even though he was smaller than most of them.

Chapter Nineteen

Freedom

FINNISH RESISTANCE GREW IN ALL AREAS. Knowing the difficulties Russian was having at home, harassment and passive resistance increased throughout Finland. The forces in Russia that were working to overthrow the tsar looked at Finland as a prize too dear.

Lenin, the leader of the communist party, spent some time in Finland hiding from his enemies in Russia. He saw first hand the stiff backbone or *sisu* of the subject Finns. He was the first to exclude Finland in their line of conquests.

In 1917 the Bolsheviks killed Tsar Nicholas and his family. The Finns saw this as the time to declare their independence, and they wasted no time in doing so.

Vilho called a meeting of the heads of each resistance group to meet at the Boar's Head in Kiivijarvi.

When all were assembled, he stood up and said, "We have declared our independence but that's not all there is to it. We have much to do to consolidate our efforts so that we do not appear to be a weak target for takeover by anyone else."

"What else is there? We are free," shouted one of the leaders with his arms spread wide.

Leslie W. Wisuri

"Declaring ourselves as free doesn't make us free. Not alone. Several of the Russian outposts say they are not going back to Russia. That includes most of the men here in Kiivijarvi. This can pose a problem if they decide to become outlaw bands. Some may want to integrate themselves into our country. Many questions arise as to who we should and should not accept.

"I say send them all back to Russia or kill them. They tortured us for so long. Let's give them a taste of their own medicine."

"I sometimes feel the same way, but if we do that we can create some big problems as the remainder turn outlaw. Think about what we did with just a few good men. Do we want to fight them or have them join us?"

The people had to think about that. Someone offered, "Well, some of them might be acceptable, but the leaders who ordered this have to go."

"Then again, you know many of those repressive orders came from St. Petersburg and Helsinki. We don't have access to those leaders and the tsar and his family are dead. Our worst leader from here, Major Rykov, is dead also."

"What do you think we ought to do?"

"I think we should start here. Each of you who have Russians in your area must do the same thing. I suggest we approach the Russians at the post and give them two choices. One, they sign a paper saying they no longer have any allegiance to Russia in any way and want to become Finnish citizens, or, the second choice is to leave for Russia immediately and never come back."

"What if they refuse to do either one?"

"We make it plain that they'll be ousted from our country by force if necessary."

"Let's do it now. I want to see the expression on some of their faces," shouted another leader.

"We have some other business," said Vilho. "They are forming a parliament in Helsinki, and each area has to be represented. I suggest we appoint leaders from each resistance area until we can get free elections going. If someone doesn't think he can handle it, I want you to suggest someone from your area who can. Obviously you are the best ones to appoint someone who will do a good job in Helsinki."

"How long before we have free elections?"

"I don't know. Soon I hope. I want you to sit down for the next hour or so and see what you come up with for representation to Helsinki. Then several of you must go with me to the post and deliver that ultimatum. I doubt they will make any decisions now, but by tomorrow we must have papers ready for them to become Finnish residents."

"What about all the weapons and food they have in their warehouses?"

"I think we ought to confiscate all of it, including the buildings. We need a place to start our own training program. Let's see how many come over to our side first. That will give us an idea how much of a fight taking the post will be. Maybe no fight at all if most of them decide to become Finns."

The men talked among themselves, and most decided to be the temporary leaders in their areas. Two said they didn't know enough about making laws and such but they did have some others in mind for their area.

Vilho picked Jacob Korpi and Waino Koski to go with him to deliver the message to the men at the post. They rigged a white flag of truce so they wouldn't be shot.

Waino voiced concern. "They might detain you or shoot you even though we are under a flag of truce."

"I doubt that. I'm sure they'll want to know where they stand in the community and with us. They might shoot us afterwards, but I doubt that, too."

The three of them walked to the post gate and were stopped by two guards.

Vilho said, "We are here to talk to your commander."

"We have orders to stop everyone but Russians from entering."

"Fine. One of you go to headquarters and tell the commandant we are here to talk."

One guard took off at a run while the other watched warily from his guard house, his rifle trained on the men.

"They must feel very insecure at the guard house to have two guards," said Vilho quietly to the others.

Shortly the guard came back with six other Russians. They searched the three Finns thoroughly.

"We have to be sure you're not carrying any kind of weapons to do our people harm."

"How much harm could the three of us do to your people," said Vilho scornfully.

"We are just following orders."

The two guards stayed while the other six herded them toward headquarters. Gerchenoff and Kalashnikov met them at the door and politely invited them in. They had set up a table and chairs in the main orderly room. Vilho could not help but notice that the other office doors were slightly ajar. Vilho was sure there were armed men behind both doors. Gerchenoff asked them to sit down. When they were seated he and Kalashnikov sat down.

"What's on your mind, Vilho?" asked Gerchenoff.

"It's not so much what's on our mind as what's on your mind and what are your intentions now that we have the upper hand and freedom declared?"

Kalashnikov took no part in the discussion even though he was the ranking commander. Vilho got the feeling he was not going to commit until he had some time to think about it.

"We have no orders from anyone back in Russia. Helsinki has told us to sit tight, but many of our men are reluctant to return to Russia if orders come to do that. I have not made up my mind either way. I'm a soldier; I'm used to waiting for orders. Given a choice, I'll probably go back to Russia if everything is stable. Right now it looks like so much turmoil that I doubt that there will be a place for me. I'd like to stay here, but I know there'll be much resentment."

"That's true," said Vilho slowly, "but you can settle somewhere else where they don't know you, I understand that Rykov was behind a lot of the orders that made our lives miserable. Our first thought is to return in kind, but then we would be just like you."

"I'm sorry for the many things that went on over the years."

"Your apology is accepted. We have two choices for you and your men. One, you become citizens of Finland and renounce all loyalties to Russia. Number two, you return to Russia immediately and don't come back. You may convey this message to your men. We'll be back tomorrow with papers for those who want to stay. We intend to take over this post and all the supplies stored here."

"I don't know if I'll allow that last part."

"You have no choice. We'll take it by force if necessary. You have a very small group and not all of them fighters. We could take you easily. You can report that you were overwhelmed by a superior force and by surprise. I would prefer this to fighting as there has been enough bloodshed."

"How long do we have to think about all this?"

"Until noon tomorrow."

"Until noon then," said Kalashnikov, rising.

Vilho, Jacob, and Waino left for town.

"That went smoother than I thought it would," said Waino.

"It's not over yet. I worry about Kalashnikov not saying a word. He may decide to fight for the post," said Jacob.

"Kalashnikov won't fight. Mika has been talking to him a lot, and he thinks he is very much for our cause even though he hasn't said anything for sure."

"I'll believe it when I see it," said Jacob.

Gerchenoff and Kalashnikov looked at each other wanting the other one to speak first. A long few minutes elapsed before Gerchenoff asked, "You outrank me, what do you think?"

"It looks like we have to go their way or get killed. The decision is up to everyone individually. I think when we give the choice to our men, we'll have an even smaller fighting force.

Personally, I am going to sign the paper. I'm not sure if I'll stay here or go back to Helsinki, but I've become good friends with Mika and like this area very well. The problem is what will I do for a living? All I know is soldiering."

"That's all I know myself."

"The Finns are going to need trained soldiers to build up their army. I don't know if they will have me, but I intend to offer my services."

The next morning Kalashnikov presented the Finnish proposal to his men.

"I want you to know that there'll be no repercussions in any way, no matter what you decide. I'm telling you that I'm going to try to stay and be a part of the Finnish army if they'll have me. Captain Gerchenoff has made the same decision."

At noon on that same day Vilho returned with Mika, Jacob, and Waino. All but two of the remaining men opted to stay and become a part of Finland.

Vilho said to Kalashnikov and Gerchenoff, "I appreciate your decision not to shed any more blood. Your decision to become part of our army is great. I can't make that final decision, but I'm sure that my recommendation to accept you will carry some weight."

Vilho sent Jacob to get more of his people to occupy the post. The takeover went smoothly, with the Russians helping as much as they could. A few weeks later, Vilho received word that he could use any Russian military personnel who wanted to become part of the Finnish army.

Vilho put Kalashnikov in charge of his same old post. Gerchenoff decided to go to another post. The situation had come full circle. Peace and freedom for which Vilho and Jonas before him had fought so hard finally began to fill the land.

Chapter Twenty

Full Circle

Vilho had been corresponding with Jonas in America. Jonas was also keeping up to date on all the events taking place in his beloved Finland.

Jonas and Emma decided to go back for a visit after Finland was free of the Russian yoke. They planned it as a visit only as they had come to love their adopted country. They had two children. Their eldest, Vilho, was, of course, named after their dear friend in Finland; their daughter had been named Lily.

In his time in America, Jonas had carved a nice farm out of the wilderness in northern Michigan. He farmed in the summer and worked in lumber camps in the winter to pay off the farm sooner.

The decision to go to Finland had been difficult as they hated to leave their home. A neighbor agreed to watch the farm while they were away. They left in the fall after all the harvesting had been completed and hoped to be back before severe weather set in.

The children enjoyed the train trip and boat ride. This was their first trip away from home.

Vilho met them in Helsinki with a team of horses and a new buggy. It was a five-day trip to Kiivijarvi. Each night they stayed with people Vilho knew. Everyone was glad to see

Jonas, who had been the flint that had started the Finnish fight for freedom. The trip might have gone quicker if everyone had not insisted on a big party at each stop. Vilho was partly to blame for this as he was trying to make Jonas welcome and want to remain in Finland.

Both Emma and Jonas were getting impatient with the protracted trip and wanted to get to Kiivijarvi to see their friends and family. All this socializing began to wear on them. Emma was especially anxious to see her mother, father, and brother.

A joyous reunion was held at the Lehtinen house when the group finally arrived. Mary and Marty were there. Marti was the same age as Lily, and they got along well. Vilho, Jonas' eldest, distained younger set. He thought he should be included in the adult group.

Vilho said to Jonas, "I know you were going to make this a visit only. I've been hoping to convince you to stay. We need men like you to help run this county."

"It's very flattering that you would want me. It's a hard decision, and I've thought about it ever since we've arrived here. It's doubly hard seeing everyone at peace and no Russians to contend with. Our beautiful country is free at last. But Emma and I have put down roots in America. I think we should go back. We have come to love America as much or more than Finland. Too much time has passed since we left here. It would be too hard to start all over again."

"You could sell the farm back there and buy another one here."

"I suppose so, but I'm not going to do that." Jonas said this with finality and conviction. "You're doing a good job here, and the people really respect you. I'm sure you'll continue to do a good job without my help."

Vilho was disappointed by this, but he tried to understand.

Jonas and his family stayed another two weeks, then, quietly, they returned to their Michigan farm in America.